ALL YOU NEED IS LOVE

NYENGI KOIN

Originally published in 1987 by Macmillan Nigeria
Limited

Copyright © 1986 Nyengi Koin
Reprint edition by NEOBOOKS 2018

NEOANCESTORIES@GMAIL.COM

ISBN: 979-8-89693-041-9

CONTENTS

For Auntie Deigha

Thank you for all your love and care.

CHAPTER ONE

The door to the Beatons' sitting room flew open. Marie Beaton looked up from her magazine, then smiled affectionately at her daughter. Tokoni was beaming, her lovely eyes sparkling with excitement.

"Hello, Toks. What's up?" she asked fondly, smiling too.

Tokoni ran from the door and enveloped her mother in a big hug. "Guess what has happened."

Marie Beaton could hardly breathe. She pushed her daughter away gently and said with a warm and loving smile, "You are hurting me, my dear. How can I guess, when you are holding me so tight?"

Tokoni laughed and released her mother. She felt she was going to burst with the weight of her happiness soon if she did not tell anyone her news. But she would keep her dear mother a little more in suspense and give her three guesses.

"Well now, let me think," her mother said, catching the excitement in the young girl's voice. "You've won first prize in the raffle or the lottery."

"Mummy, you know I don't play any of those things. Try again."

The mother looked at her daughter's radiant face. "You've been promoted?"

"No, Mummy, you are wrong again. Hmm, you think it's that easy to get a promotion? I was promoted only six months ago. Now, you have just one more guess."

"Third time lucky," smiled her mother. "Let me see." She thought for a couple of seconds and exclaimed, "Now I know! That tooth of yours!"

Tokoni laughed out loud and sank onto a chair opposite her mother. What a guess! She had even forgotten she had a problem tooth in the excitement of the day. "No, you are wrong again. Close your eyes and let me show you." She held out her left hand. "Now, look!"

Marie Beaton opened her eyes, but the smile froze on her face. She stared at the ring. It was a plain gold band, with diamonds clustered around a beautiful sapphire. It was a lovely ring. In the light of the sun, its sparkling diamonds quite dazzled and confused her. She dragged her eyes away and looked at her daughter.

"Tolu and I are engaged. You are the first person we are telling," Tokoni said with a tremor in her voice. The shocked look on her mother's face at the sight of the ring on her finger had taken her happiness away as fast as lightning.

"You are joking, Tokoni!"

"It's no joke, Mummy."

"But you can't, Tokoni! How could you?" said her mother in a shocked tone of voice, as if Tokoni had told her she had committed some crime.

"What's so wrong about our getting engaged?" Tokoni stared at her mother.

"What's wrong with it?" her mother snapped. "All these foreign romances you've been reading must have gone to your head! How can you tell me you've got engaged this way?"

"I'm sorry, but Tolu..."

"And anyway," her mother cut in angrily, "hasn't he enough respect to come and greet me after giving my daughter an engagement ring?"

Tokoni sighed. Both of them had feared some opposition. That was why they had decided to get engaged before telling anybody. She had been so happy when Tolu had slipped the ring on her finger and told her he would always love her. It was just as she had read in all those novels and seen in films, and she had thought nothing could take away her happiness. This was her mother spoiling it for her.

"He wanted to come in with me, Mummy, but I told him not to. I wanted to tell you myself and hear what you have to say before involving him," she explained.

"Oh! Oh! Isn't he involved yet? Haven't you both become engaged already? You must be out of your mind to think you can marry a Yoruba boy anyway," her mother said coldly.

"Oh, so that's what you are shocked about," said Tokoni quietly, raising her eyebrows. "Is that all you have against him? But I've been going out with Tolu for ages, and you have never raised any serious objections before."

"I did not know you were so serious about him," her mother replied. "I thought you were sensible, Tokoni. You know you are my first-born. You are not setting a good example to your brother and sister."

"Mummy, you should have no worry on that score. Elaye is likely to marry an Ijaw. We are not all going away from home," Tokoni said, her lower lip trembling.

Marie Beaton got up from her chair. She did not quite know what to say. She had set her heart on both her daughters marrying Ijaws. She would not be bothered much if her only son, Pere, got married to a girl from any part of the world, as he would still be bringing his bride and children home to his village. But daughters were quite different. They would be taken away, and their children would hardly know they had roots in Ijawland. All the years she'd lived in Lagos, she had always made sure that her children associated with Ijaws, made sure that they did not forget their roots.

"What have you got against him anyway, except that he is Yoruba?" Tokoni's voice broke into her thoughts. "I thought you were not a tribalist. I suppose it is different when it comes to your own child! Were you not the one who talked to

Bindo's parents to let her marry Ete?"

Tokoni did not know what to think. When her cousin Bindo had insisted on marrying Ete, an Itsekiri boy, her mother had been the one who had helped Bindo. She had spoken to her brother and sister-in-law, arguing so reasonably that no one today chose husbands for their daughters. Did this mean her mother was a hypocrite, setting different standards for her own children and her brother's children? Even as the thought occurred to her, she dismissed it. Her mother was a very sincere person. She had genuinely felt Bindo's sorrow when she had a baby on the way and could not marry Ete. "What's the difference between Tolu and Ete?"

Her mother went and sat by her side. "Look, Tokoni," she said, "I have nothing against him personally, but he is above you. He is a doctor, and his family and friends will look down on you and tell him he could have chosen better. It will be tough for you, and you will be unhappy..."

"What about you and Daddy?" Tokoni interrupted coldly. "He was a doctor and you were a caterer, and yet you were happy. I don't see much difference between a caterer and a secretary, I really don't!"

"Our case was quite different. We came from the same place, and those days you could hardly find educated Ijaw girls, so your father did not look down on me. He was proud of me..."

"Tolu is proud of me, too, whatever you say.

And anyway, how do you know that if I marry an Ijaw, there won't be any problem? Hasn't it happened before?" Tokoni queried.

Her mother sighed. She knew it was almost useless explaining to Tokoni, as she had set her heart on marrying this boy. But there was no harm in trying to dissuade her. At least she would have the consolation that she had tried.

"Tokoni, my dear. We have been through all that before. I am not saying the same can't happen with an Ijaw boy. But when you marry someone from your own place, he respects you because he knows your background. He knows the family you come from and what they are. And his people, too, won't want to offend yours. There will be respect on both sides. It's your happiness I want. I know you think you love Tolu, but that's not all that matters. His family won't want to support you in a family council because you will be more or less an outsider."

"I don't think, Mummy, that I love him. I am quite sure about that. And what girl, marrying into any family, isn't an outsider?" demanded Tokoni, breaking into a sob. "Why can't you just accept him for my sake? You always say it's my happiness you want. Do you think I will be happy married to somebody I don't love or who doesn't love me?"

"But, Tokoni, am I asking you to marry someone you don't love? I am merely asking you to consider this carefully for your own good. I don't think you realize the things you will have to put up with—quarrels, disapproval, and all that—if you marry into any other tribe. The fact that you can speak their language and understand a lot of their customs does not make any difference. He will not speak your language. He will never really understand you or even want to." Marie Beaton put her hands on her daughter's shoulders and her eyes pleaded with the young girl.

Tokoni said nothing, just stared at her mother with tears in her eyes.

"I have seen people who have had to bear a lot of suffering because of inter-tribal marriages. Why don't you wait for some time? It's not as if you are getting old. Wait a year or two. You will get over Tolu. There is nothing one can't get over, my child. It only takes time. And love is what you make of it. You might fall in love with a nice young Ijaw boy yet. Look at Ebitimi Ifie, for instance. He is madly in love with you. Why not give him a chance, my dear?" she concluded pleadingly.

This was about the longest speech Tokoni had ever heard from her mother. Ebitimi Ifie was the eldest son of a friend of one of Tokoni's uncles. He wasn't bad looking, just twenty-five, and had a first-rate job in his father's big furniture factory. Along with his three brothers, he would eventually be one of the directors. He had been in love with Tokoni for the past eighteen months and hung about with a stubborn devotion. He was cheerful, generous, and full of fun. Everybody liked him, but Tokoni had eyes only for Tolu. She was fond of Ebitimi, but only as one would be of a favorite elder brother.

"Mummy, you are just being selfish. How can I make you understand that it's Tolu I love and want to marry? You are mistaken if you think I will marry Ebitimi Ifie. He may be madly in love with me, but I am not in love with him. There is nothing I can do about it. I don't care if his father is rich and Uncle Charles' friend or not. I don't care if Tolu hasn't got a kobo to his name. I love him. I can and will endure anything for him."

"Tokoni, please understand. I am..."

"I have always tried my best to please you. This is the only time I am really begging you for a favor, asking you for something which is the whole of my life. You know what is best for me! You'll deny me this happiness!" Tokoni ran out of the room.

Marie Beaton sat stunned. She was almost in tears herself. She knew this daughter of hers so well. There was very little she could do. This was one time Tokoni was going to have her own way. Right from a baby, Tokoni had been a very affectionate girl whose heart ruled her head. That was the weak point that made her most vulnerable. When she loved, it would be forever. Marie knew Tokoni would love a man completely and without restraint only once. It was a common trait in the women of her family. They were all one-man women who loved with their heart, body, and soul.

Marie was still a beautiful woman of average height. She had become a bit plump after her third and last baby, but she was still lovely. Her three children, especially the two girls, had inherited her fine looks and a lot of her good nature. She knew what love and happiness in a marriage were like. Hers had been a paradise, a heaven on earth, and she wished her children could one day know the same joy.

"If only Stephen were alive today," she thought distractedly. "He could have taken this problem in his stride. He would have known what to do. He was so good at handling difficulties."

It was not that she disliked Tolu. He was nice enough, but even though she knew him as Tokoni's boyfriend, she had refused to attach any importance to the relationship. She liked to think she was broad-minded, but even now, tribalism reigned supreme. The people from the majority areas still looked down on the people from the so-called minority areas. The Yoruba especially regarded themselves as the first-class citizens, the builders of the nation. Many of them classified everybody else as "kobokobo." They would not tolerate any child of theirs marrying a "kobokobo."

Perhaps she was being selfish and unfair. She knew practically nothing about Tolu's family. Being educated and enlightened people, they probably had a broader outlook and a better attitude to people from other tribes. Those ideas about the Yoruba being better than "kobokobo" were widespread among the lesser educated who had not seen much of the country. Tolu's people were probably not like that. Whether they were or not, it wouldn't be all honey and roses for Tokoni, she knew.

One thought after another ran in the mother's mind, but one was uppermost: She must try further. She mustn't give up. "It was always better to stick to one's own kind," she said to herself. Any marriage at all had enough problems of its own without having to add discrimination. Tokoni would thank her for it in the long run, she was sure.

She got up and went to Tokoni's room. She turned the knob, but the door was locked. She knocked, but there was no answer, so she knew the girl must be crying. Tokoni's tears, as they had always teased her, were just inside her eyelids. Marie went to her own bedroom and sank down wearily on a chair.

Tokoni, crying as if her heart would break, heard her mother knocking on the door and calling to her, but she did not answer. Her life would be incomplete without Tolu. She could not begin to imagine life without him. He was the first, the only, and the last for her, and nothing her mother said would change that. It was all right for her mother to say she would fall in love with a nice young Ijaw boy. Not that she had anything against Ijaw boys. If only she had met the right one before meeting Tolu... but now it was too late. She did not know of anyone who could stand comparison with Tolu. She loved her mother very much, and they'd all been very close since their father died. But oh, no! She couldn't leave Tolu. It would be throwing the last six years of her life away as well as all her future.

"Hello, Tokoni. Are you there?" Elaye's voice came through the closed door and brought Tokoni's weeping to an abrupt end.

Tokoni got up and opened the door, and Elaye, the tomboy of the family, bounced through in her characteristic way. "What did you lock the door for? I was going to..." She stopped suddenly as she saw her elder sister's tear-stained face. "Tokoni, what is it?" she inquired, all concern, and Tokoni burst into fresh sobs. "Hello, Mummy. What's the matter with her?"

"She's engaged to Tolu and..."

"Is that why she's crying? I should think she would be laughing, not crying!" Elaye interrupted.

"Yes, but I have not..."

"Oh Mummy! You don't mean you said she could not marry Tolu. I can't believe it!" Mrs. Beaton nodded.

Elaye sighed in exasperation. "You know they both love each other. Why don't you want them to get married?"

"Because he is Yoruba!" Tokoni supplied, talking for the first time since her sister came into the room.

"Surely you are not bothered by that? You appeared to like Tolu. Why did you think they've been going out together for so long?" Elaye demanded.

Marie Beaton sat on the edge of the bed and sighed. She did not know how to begin to explain to these two young girls that it was not Tolu himself she was against. She liked Tolu. He was a nice, very polite young man, but though she had always welcomed him to their house with genuine warmth and happiness, she had never thought of him as a potential son-in-law. She knew he was Tokoni's friend, but it had never occurred to her that Tokoni was so much in love with him. All three of her children had so many friends. How naive could she get? She had thought they were just good friends, going out together for the fun of it, until they each met the right person for them and were ready for marriage. But of course, she should have realized that at twenty-two, Tokoni was on the threshold of marriage.

"Elaye, my dear," she said, "I don't have anything against Tolu, as I've already told Tokoni. But she won't find it easy marrying into another tribe. The fact that she understands Yoruba is of no importance. There'll be so much disappointment and disapproval, so much unhappiness."

"It can happen if she marries an Ijaw too, you know. Happiness all depends on the family and individuals."

"Yes, and you know it, Mummy. That's what I said," Tokoni put in.

"I know. But assuming you go and live in his hometown and the family starts maltreating you, how do we know?" Mrs. Beaton demanded, knowing fully well it was such a feeble protest. Still, she had to say something.

"There is no distant hometown to go and live in. Tolu is from Lagos State. I'm not going to be maltreated, if that's what you are scared about. I am old enough to take care of myself," Tokoni assured her mother.

"You are not being fair. You married for love yourself, so you should know how Tokoni is feeling," Elaye rejoined.

Marie sighed again. Oh, yes, she had married very much for love. She had been born in Burutu but did not remember much of her life out there before they moved to Port Harcourt. There she was the local beauty, the cream of the society she moved in, and was sought by young and old alike. Although she could have had her pick of the men, she had fallen in love with a young doctor whom she met quite accidentally. He had shown not the least interest in her at first.

"Yes," she said, "I know how she is feeling. But, Tokoni, what do Tolu's family think about it? I mean, what did they say?"

"Mummy, I don't know yet. Tolu is going to tell them this evening, and tomorrow when we meet, he'll tell me what they said."

"But what do they think of you already? I mean, how do they treat you now?" her mother pursued.

A worried frown, which both her mother and her sister did not fail to notice, creased Tokoni's brow. "Hmm, Mummy, I don't even know. They hardly talk to me whenever I go to their house. They just seem indifferent to me. Whenever I catch their eyes, I can always read the feeling of coolness... reserve... distance... in them." Tokoni paused and glanced at her mother to see her reaction.

Her mother's face was expressionless, but she nodded her head.

Tokoni continued slowly, "They make me feel stupid. I never know what to say or do to please them. Anyway, Tolu and I are going to watch *The Gods Are Not To Blame* at the Glover Hall tomorrow. I'll know what their reaction is then." Tokoni paused again, toying with the ring on her finger. "The rest of his family are the same—indifferent—but they tolerate me better than his parents do. They don't watch my every move. They scare me, Tolu's parents..."

Mrs. Beaton looked at Elaye and nodded her head slowly. "You see what I mean? Did I know about all these things before I said his family won't stand by you in a family council? I've heard so much, and I don't want any of you to suffer."

"Mummy, Tokoni could have lied to you. She could have said they all liked her or did not mind, just to get your consent, but she did not. Do you know why?" Elaye paused for effect and then continued, "She loves you and does not want to keep anything from you. We all know it's our happiness you are concerned about. Don't you think this is a risk Tokoni has to take?"

"Elaye, you don't know what you are talking about..."

"Mummy, please let me finish. Tokoni has made her bed. You have to let her lie on it. You don't know that Tolu's parents will refuse their approval. They might realize how much this means to their son. And anyway, even if they don't, it won't do for Toks to meet opposition right from her home. She could have a lot of that from the Johnsons, and she needs all the support we can give her. Please, don't let this thing strain the love between us."

Marie Beaton nearly burst into tears. She never knew Elaye had so much knowledge of the world and good sense. She had never heard her giving such good advice to anyone. Elaye had always struck her as a tomboy who had little time to think about deep emotions. In that moment, she realized that she did not know these children of hers as well as she thought she did.

"I don't know what to say. I'm so confused. You've messed it up from the beginning, Tokoni, both of you, by getting engaged first and telling the parents later. You know how the Yoruba do this. They make such a big thing out of engagements, and of course, the parents have to be in the whole business, not just told." Marie sighed. "How I wish your father was alive!"

"Daddy would have approved. I'm sure he would have. He met Tolu twice before his death, and they liked each other," Tokoni said, her lovely, expressive eyes pleading with her mother.

"Yes. He would have been disappointed a bit, just like you, but he was such an understanding man. He wouldn't have minded too much," Elaye offered.

"And Tolu was genuinely distressed when Daddy died. Remember all he did for me? How many young men can be so thoughtful?" Tokoni mumbled.

She would never forget his kindness. He sent her a telegram, cards, letters, and also gave her some money. He came to see her very often with some friends to cheer and console them. He was like a pillar of strength to her then, always comforting her and ever conscious of her moods and needs. He knew when she did not wish to talk, and he would just sit by her side, holding her hands. He was tact itself, and she could not help thanking her stars she met him. By that time, she was hopelessly in love with him.

"I shall have to think more about this." Her mother's voice brought an abrupt end to Tokoni's reverie. "It's a very serious matter."

"All right, think about it." It was Elaye who spoke. "But remember all that advice you gave Bindo's Mummy and Uncle Ben. This is no different from Ete's case."

That night in her room, Marie Beaton could not sleep. She tossed and turned on the bed, thinking of this problem. She was the one who had told Bindo's parents not to look at the marriage as losing a daughter but as gaining a son. "Why," she wondered, "had she felt she should plead their cause? Perhaps it was because Bindo was pregnant and because Ete, being from Bendel State, was from a place a bit nearer their homeland."

If she looked at it in a broader sense, they were all Nigerians. Still, she did not want her daughter to marry a Yoruba with their superior airs. "Who was she to judge, anyway?" she reproached herself the next instant. "Wasn't she behaving in just the way she was expecting the Johnsons to behave?" As Elaye rightly said, this was one of the crises Tokoni would have to face in life. She needed all the love and support her family could give. It would be too much for Tokoni to face opposition right from her own home and then go out and probably meet cold disapproval from the Johnsons.

And then there was Stephen's family and her brothers to face. They would not all approve, she knew, but as Elaye said, she wanted nothing to come between her and the children. They all had lived so happily together until the cold hands of death had snatched Stephen away from them. All three of the children were very industrious, well-behaved, and clever, sailing through their exams. After Stephen's death, it had not been easy for her to be both father and mother. If her children had not been wonderful, understanding, and cooperative, it would have been worse. They had helped her so much, and until now, she had had no real problem with any of them. She was grateful to God for them. They were so undemanding. Suddenly, she knew what she must do. She had to stand by Tokoni. She owed her that much. First, she must know what Tolu's parents had to say. The next morning she called Tokoni and Elaye into her room. One look at Tokoni's dismal face assured her she had taken the right decision.

"Well, my dears. I'm sorry I've upset you so much, Tokoni. I was thinking only of you and what you will go through if you marry Tolu. As you've already said, his parents don't positively approve of you. I suppose we just have to keep our fingers crossed and hope they'll change their minds. You both know very well that he is the only child of his parents. They will expect quite a lot from him. They are probably expecting him to marry from one of these high-society families. I love you very much, Tokoni, and it's your happiness I want, nothing else. If you, my children, are happy, then wherever I am, I shall be happy too."

"But Mummy," broke in Tokoni, "there's nothing that will make me happier than marrying Tolu."

"I know, my dear. I fully realize that there's nothing you need from me more than my moral support at this time. I assure you that if you both love each other enough to contemplate marriage, then I'll help you all I can. But first, I have to know what his parents say. I want you to promise me that you won't rush into marriage. Think carefully about it, give it time. To choose to spend the rest of your life with someone is the biggest decision you will ever make. I know you've known each other for quite a long time, but there's a lot of difference between being boyfriend and girlfriend and being married."

Tokoni could not believe her ears. She had listened attentively to every word her mother said, but she felt as if she had not heard right. She looked questioningly at her mother, who understood her uncertainty and nodded.

Still, it was Elaye who asked, "You mean it's all right?"

"Yes," agreed their mother, "subject to what his parents say."

That was enough for Tokoni. Eyes glowing, she flung her arms around her mother, tears of joy streaming down her cheeks. "I can't believe it! You've accepted in so short a time. I was expecting more opposition."

"So was I, but I'm not surprised anyway. You are so understanding, such a wonderful person!" Elaye said happily.

"I promise you I shan't rush into anything," Tokoni said, then paused for breath and continued excitedly, "You needn't worry. I shall be blissfully happy with Tolu. He will be so pleased. Oh... I don't know how to thank you. I'm so happy!"

Marie was touched. "I'm only doing what I should have done before. I only hope it will be fine with his parents."

"So do I! Oh Mummy, it will be all right, don't

you think?" Tokoni asked, looking at her mother for reassurance.

"Of course, it will!" Elaye stated optimistically.

"I suppose so," nodded their mother. "Love always finds a way."

Tokoni hugged both her mother and sister again and walked out of the room, her heart singing. She had counted on her mother's support, but after the initial reception of the news, she had not been so sure. She thought of Tolu and anticipated the happiness and delight that would light up his face when she told him about this. She herself was so happy she could not wait to see him in the evening.

She was ready almost at the arranged time. But she did not want him to come in just yet. Somehow she did not want this fragile happiness to be shaken. If Tolu came in, her mother would surely express some of her doubts and fears. And who knows what one word could lead to? she asked herself. He must not come into this house until she knew what his parents had to say. So when Tolu hooted at the gate, she seized her bag, called goodbye, and ran out to meet him before he could negotiate the difficult entrance to the compound.

"Let's go," she said breathlessly, slipping into the seat beside him and blowing him a kiss.

CHAPTER TWO

Tolu was in no mood to enjoy any play, but, like Tokoni, he had a great sense of loyalty. He had promised her that they were going to see this play, and he was not going to let her down. That was the only reason he was there.

He felt cold all through whenever he remembered that scene with his parents at home last night. He had waited until they had finished their evening meal before announcing his engagement.

His mother was shocked. She opened her mouth, agape, and stared at him as if he had told her he had broken some kind of taboo. His father pretended not to have heard him. That had always been his way of announcing, "You don't know what you are saying," and Tolu knew it.

"Did I hear you say you are engaged?" his father asked him at last.

"Yes, Papa. I'm engaged to be married to Tokoni Beaton," Tolu replied, his voice already on the defensive.

"But, Tolulope dear..." his mother began, "you can't mean it. You did not tell us you were so serious about her."

"But, Mama, I don't think I have to tell you

before getting engaged."

"It depends on what you mean by engagement," his mother countered.

"All right. I mean before I give my promise to marry her. I have given her a ring as proof of my promise," he added.

Mrs. Johnson beat the palms of her hands together to express her astonishment. "What will everyone say when they hear this? With all the eligible, pretty young girls in this Lagos, you had to go and marry a 'kobokobo'! I shouldn't think anybody will approve."

"And what do I care about that? She might be 'kobokobo' or whatever you want to call her, but she is the girl I love. And I'm marrying her. I don't care a hoot about any other eligible girl or what anybody says, come to that," Tolu retorted. "You're not against her as a person. You don't know her and you've never tried to. You can't choose a wife for me. This is my life. Leave me to do what I like with it."

"Tolulope!" his father cut in, with that masterful tone that indicated finality.

"Yes, Papa?" Tolu asked humbly and was immediately annoyed with himself. His father's voice could make him feel so young and weak, as if he were still a mere kid.

"No son of mine, and I repeat, no son of mine," continued his father in that same voice, "is going to marry any girl that's not Yoruba. That's all I've got to say about it." With this, he got up and left the table, going into his room.

"Tolu, try to see reason," pleaded his mother, confusing. "You are a Class 4 doctor and have a fine career ahead of you. How can you stoop so low as to marry a secretary? She is not up to your educational level. She will only be a disgrace to you."

"What is wrong with marrying a secretary? What is so degrading about a doctor marrying a secretary? I am certainly not the first, and I won't be the last," Tolu said coldly.

"At least, not that girl, who hasn't got anything to say for herself. She is below you both socially and educationally. Why, I can count all the words she's ever said all the times she's been to this house. She will not be able to keep up with your progress, that girl. You will soon get bored with her..."

"I haven't, during the past six years," Tolu reflected.

"I know, but it will be different when you live in the same house. She is so dull and quiet. She doesn't even share your interests or enthusiasms. That girl has..."

"Oh, Mama, please stop calling her 'that girl.' Her name is Tokoni. She is shy, and she doesn't talk much as a rule. But shall I tell you why she doesn't talk when she comes here? It's because you scare her. You make it clear you have no time for her.

You have never given her a chance."

"Did she tell you that?" his mother asked sharply.

"Tokoni?" Tolu shook his head. "Anyone with eyes will see that's how you behave to her. And you are mistaken if you think we don't share the same interests. We both love music, art, books, and films. The only thing I love and she has no enthusiasm for is going to parties."

"Now, look at the way you went and got engaged. Is that the way you saw other people do it? Don't you want to have a nice engagement like all your cousins did before you? You will lose traditional and cultural advantages if you marry this girl, Tolu. In fact, you have already started to lose good things from our tradition and custom," Tolu's mother stated.

"Mama, I love Tokoni. I don't want to concern myself with any cultural or traditional advantages," Tolu replied.

"You might think so now, my son, but cultural ties are more important as a man matures. This Tokoni girl will not fit in our community of families. I don't think she will be accepted at all."

"Then the community of families can forget Tolu because I won't give Tokoni up," Tolu declared. "I wonder why you think I've been going out with her all these years if I don't intend to marry her?"

"But Tolu, is she pregnant or what? You are our only son. It will be most humiliating for us if you marry a 'kobokobo'," his mother pleaded with him. "They are very wicked people, I tell you, and I am talking from experience."

"Not this one, Mama, not Tokoni. She is a great girl—kind, sympathetic, and good-natured. She is not pregnant. I just want to marry her, that's all. You will like her if you care to get to know her. You couldn't get a better daughter-in-law, I tell you," Tolu told his mother, half angry and half pleading in his turn.

But nothing could convince his mother. She began to cry. His father returned and began to shout. Tolu answered back angrily. This morning, they'd all just pretended as if yesterday had not happened at all, and it had left him more furious than ever.

He started the car as soon as Tokoni came in, his worries vanishing momentarily at the sight of her lovely, smiling face. She was very happy, and he tried to be flippant with her. "You look great," he said. "I like your dress. I just hope you aren't planning to ditch me at the theatre. What are the glad rags in aid of?"

"You said it, not me. Actually, I was thinking of ditching you as soon as I had the opportunity," Tokoni laughed at him.

"Very funny indeed!" Tolu said with mock severity. "Now, get down. We are not going anywhere."

"Hmm, silly," Tokoni laughed. "You know I could never do that. Oh, Tolu, my mother approves of our engagement, but she wants to know what your parents said. She was upset at first, but Elaye helped me to talk to her, and she realized there was nothing she could do about it. She has offered all her help."

Tokoni stopped and really looked at Tolu for the first time since she came into the car, searching his face to see his reaction. His face was expressionless, but she saw the hurt in his eyes and knew instinctively that he did not have a similar story to tell.

"Toks darling, they took it badly. There was the hell of a row. Anyway, I told them quite frankly that I am not bothered if they approve or not. I am old enough to get married without their consent. I know what I'm doing. For all I care, if they don't want you as their daughter-in-law, too bad. They can go to hell. I will go ahead with my plans, and they will see if I can't manage without them."

Tokoni's heart sank at Tolu's words. Before she came to the scene, Tolu and his parents had gotten on quite well. "Tolu, don't talk like that. You are talking about your parents, and you know I don't like to hear people swear."

"Sorry," he replied stubbornly. "But I am so mad with them."

"Remember you are their only child. You were

very close before. You can't just turn your back on all the good times you will have with them in the future. Give them time. I'm sure they'll come around."

"Tokoni, when will you stop thinking of others and put yourself first, huh? You really are an angel, and I love you very much," Tolu said, feeling so bad that he was causing her so much unhappiness. "I will do as you say, but I won't wait for too long."

Tokoni really was a great girl, he thought. Looking back on the few times she'd been to his house, he could remember his parents avoiding her as if she had some terrible infectious disease. They never missed an opportunity to show their disapproval, whereas her people had always welcomed him to their house and made him feel part of their family. He had never taken her to his house in the early days of their friendship, when they were still at school, but he went to her house regularly. She could not have been to his house more than ten times, yet she never complained about how his parents treated her. In her place, if he was being treated so shabbily by her family, he would have complained. "She really is a great girl," he said to himself a second time. "Anybody who thinks I will not go ahead with this wedding simply because of any tribal sentiments has to think again. They can all wait until they know what they are missing."

"If you don't feel in the mood for the theatre," she began, "would you rather we went back home?"

Tolu thought of Mrs. Beaton waiting with her anxious questions. "No," he assured her. "The play will be just the tonic I need."

The Gods Are Not To Blame turned out to be one of the best plays either of them had ever seen. Tolu could understand why Femi Robinson was always associated with it. He put all his being into the role he was playing. The auditorium was packed, and nearly all the women shed a tear or two. It was such a tragedy, and Tokoni, who was very emotional, found herself still crying as the lights came on at the end of the play. On the way home, Tolu teased Tokoni about her weeping. "That is one of the reasons why I love you," he said. "You take other people's worries for your own."

"The play was so sad," Tokoni smiled shakily.

Abruptly, they stopped talking, and a heavy silence fell like a barrier between them. Tokoni, who was sitting by the window, heaved a sigh, and tears trickled again down her cheeks.

Tolu saw them. He took her hand and squeezed it. "Don't cry, Toks, please. I promise you everything will be all right."

Tokoni fumbled blindly in her bag for a handkerchief, and as she did so, her bracelet caught the clasp of her bag. She tried to remove it, but the tears had blurred her vision. Tolu saw her difficulty and had to swerve the car into a corner. He helped her unhook the bracelet, and the words, "I love you," sparkled at Tokoni as if reassuring her. This

gold bracelet was her twenty-first birthday present
from Tolu, and she valued it above any of her other
possessions. Tolu was always giving her presents,
little things he knew she liked. Even the
handkerchief she brought out now was from him.

Tolu was very upset himself. He did not know
what to do. Like most men, he hated the sight of a
woman crying. It embarrassed him and always left
him at a loss for what to do. He squeezed her hand
again and started the car. He was glad they were
getting near her house because he knew she needed
to be alone. This tearful Tokoni disturbed his peace
of mind too much. He loved his parents and wanted
them to share in his future life, but he could not
begin to imagine life without Tokoni. He was not
going to give her up for all the prejudice in the
world. It was as if all his life she'd been around, her
serenity giving him strength and willpower. All
those years ago, he had been drawn to this girl. Why
couldn't his parents just accept facts?

"Would you like me to come in with you?" he
asked Tokoni when they got to her house. Really,
he ought to see Tokoni's mother, but if there were to
be another emotional scene, he didn't know what
might happen.

She helped him ease his conscience by shaking
her head. "No, I'd like to be alone, please, if you
don't mind. I'm sorry for breaking down like that. It
was just... Oh, I don't know. Good night, Tolu. See
you tomorrow!"

He took her hands and squeezed them gently

yet again. She had told him sometime before that the gesture always made her feel better. She managed to give Tolu a watery smile and got out of the car quickly before she could burst into tears again. She ran up the drive to her house. Tolu watched her go in and then drove off.

Tokoni let herself in and found her mother sewing in the sitting room. "Are you back? How was the play?" her mother greeted her before she could say a word. "I was just finishing the hem of this dress. Elaye is the laziest girl I know. She doesn't know how to thread a needle, yet she will worry me till I finish a dress for her the very day she wants to put it on."

"Fine!"

Marie Beaton's head, which was all the while bent on her sewing as she talked, shot up at once. She knew that muffled voice meant Tokoni had been crying. "What's wrong, Tokoni? What happened?"

Tokoni buried her head in her mother's lap as she had always done as a little girl.

"Come on, cry out. It won't do you any good to cry inside like that," Marie coaxed. "You'll soon feel better."

Tokoni took her mother's advice and cried until she was exhausted.

Then her mother said, "Now, Tokoni, you've had more than your fair share of tears since yesterday. Do you want to tell me about it? Maybe I can help. It might make you feel better to talk about it. If you'd rather not, then you'd better go to bed. You have to go to work tomorrow, you know."

Tokoni cleaned her face and explained. "Mummy, it's Tolu's parents. They were furious to hear of our engagement. He did not tell me exactly how it went, but it must have been very bad for him to be so upset."

"I'm very sorry, my dear," was all her mother could say.

"Why do they hate me so? Why? I haven't done anything wrong to them. Why are they so sure I won't make their son a good wife?" Tokoni asked dejectedly. "Why can't they give me a chance?"

Marie Beaton looked at her beautiful young daughter and wished fervently that there was some way in which she could reassure her. Tokoni was such a good-natured and well-behaved girl, not at all spoiled. Everyone who knew her loved her. Marie wished she could say something to bring a smile to her daughter's troubled face. "I don't know all the answers, my dear," she said truthfully. "Don't worry. If Tolu is really the man for you, everything will come out right in the end. It's just one of those things. I'm sure if they know you better, they will like you. All the same, Tokoni, you can't have everybody liking you."

Tokoni was grateful for these few words of comfort, but they only brought a shadow of a smile on her face.

"There's something Ina used to say to me when I was a young girl and I thought I had problems. It goes—'Stay but till tomorrow and your present sorrow will be weary and will lie down to rest.' Maybe tomorrow will bring something good," her mother comforted her.

Ina was the familiar word for mother in Ijawland. Marie and all her brothers called their mother Ina, and that was the name all the grandchildren called the venerable old lady.

Tokoni hugged her mother. "Oh Mummy, you are marvelous. You didn't even say, 'I told you so.' Poor Tolu, it must be really tough on him."

"That's my daughter," smiled Mrs. Beaton, "thinking of others even in your own distress. And did you imagine I was joking when I said I'll help you all I can? I don't like the idea of you marrying anyone who isn't Ijaw. But I like Tolu. He isn't just anyone. And if he'll make you happy, I'm willing to ignore my misgivings and give you my blessing."

"Oh Mummy, how can I thank you enough?" Tokoni breathed.

"By being the good girl you've always been. I'll continue to pray for you. To my knowledge, it's the only way I can help you. Now, find something to eat and go to bed. Remember, tears may endure for a night, but joy comes in the morning."

"Thank you, Mummy, but I'm not hungry. I am

very proud of you. You are the best mother on earth, and I wouldn't exchange you for all the world," she declared.

"Except for Tolu," her mother joked.

Ah no, Tokoni thought as she undressed for bed; she could not exchange Tolu for all the world. She never contemplated leaving him for someone else. She knew he was as much in love with her as she was with him. Everything he did showed how very much he cared for her. She always felt so safe and secure with him. He made her feel she really belonged to him, presenting her to his friends with enviable pride. Tolu was confident, very sure of himself, and masterful, and she was very proud of him.

They had started those days by writing to each other, just short, friendly notes at first. But soon, the short, friendly notes developed into long, intimate love letters. He never asked her outright to be his girlfriend, like most people do. She would never have been able to say yes. The attraction between them was mutual, so they just drifted into it, and there was hardly any need for bringing that subject up. Gradually they started going out together, and though she disliked parties, she went with him all the same. She was the odd one out for this in her family. Her parents, Elaye, and Pere, were ready for a party any day. They simply adored dancing and teased her that she had two left feet. That was why she could not dance. She loved being with Tolu. It made her feel good. Their dates were mainly going to films and plays.

"Stay but till tomorrow and your present sorrow will be weary and will lie down to rest," her mother had said. Oh God, how she wished this would turn out to be true. If she knew Tolu's parents, they would go to any lengths to see that they had their way; if only they could come to see her as a person. She was determined to look on the bright side of things. She would be optimistic, and as her mother said, maybe tomorrow would bring pleasant news. To assure herself that everything would be all right tomorrow, she sang the hymn her mother had quoted earlier. By the time she had finished singing, she felt more confident and fell asleep almost immediately.

In spite of her confidence and her mother's reassurance, however, Tokoni could not sleep much. She awoke very early the next morning. It was strange, but she had dreamt that Tolu was being taken away from her, and she was running after him, begging whoever was taking him away to leave him alone, but however much she tried, she could not reach them.

"Oh God," she thought as she got up from the bed, "please let it be all right. This means so much to me. I think I'll go crazy if things continue this way, as bad as they must have been in Tolu's house yesterday. I don't know how I can bear it." She studied her reflection critically, wondering whether there was any great change in her. Already, the situation was telling on her. She looked and felt like someone enduring great stress. She studied herself again and wondered if there was any reason, apart from the fact that she was not Yoruba, why Tolu's parents thought she would not make him a good wife. She thought of Tolu's words again, that he could not care less whether they disowned him or not, and shuddered. It would be too great a price for him to pay, and she did not want that for him. He and his parents, although they had not been particularly close in earlier years, had gotten on well before they knew about her and things became complicated.

There was always some undercurrent that Tokoni sensed but could not make contact with whenever she met any of Tolu's large family. There was one occasion when Tolu had been telling her about a funny incident. She had shared his laughter for a moment, and then encountering his mother's speculative gaze, was silenced sheepishly.

Suddenly, she felt a headache that threatened to blind her with pain. Wearily she went to the bathroom and took a cold bath, washing her forehead over and over again with the cold water. She tried to empty her mind of all confused thoughts as she finished her bath and lay quiet and relaxed on her bed until the headache had gone. It had only been tension that had brought it on, and it went away just as suddenly as it came.

She said, "Good morning" to her sister who had just got up and related the whole incident to her.

Elaye's face went through a number of rapid changes. "It will be all right, Tokoni, don't worry. It will be all right."

"I hope so, Elaye, but you know, Tolu's family treat him as someone special. His father is the youngest child in a family of six. It's the same with his mother. She is the youngest of two boys and two girls," Tokoni said and then paused, to speak about it.

Elaye said nothing. She knew Tokoni needed to talk about it.

"All their brothers and sisters got married before them. So Tolu is the youngest grandchild of both sets of grandparents. And you know what that means. They all dote on him—cousins, uncles, aunties, grandparents. You know how he will feel if they all turn against him," she finished.

"Toks, it will be all right."

"Amen," Tokoni laughed. "Well, I'd better let you get ready for school, Elaye," she added, getting up from the bed.

Elaye smiled at her and went out.

CHAPTER THREE

The phone had been ringing for some time before Mrs. Beaton picked it up. She had been busy making foofoo in the kitchen. She hated leaving her foofoo half-done for something else, once she had started making it, because it brought out unwanted lumps if she did.

"Hello?" she said, automatically giving the number.

"Hello," came a woman's voice from the other end. "Can I speak to Mrs. Beaton—Tokoni's mother, please? This is Mrs. Johnson—Tolu Johnson's mother."

"Oh, how are you, Ma? I'm sorry I kept you waiting on the line. I was busy in the kitchen," explained Mrs. Beaton politely.

"You must know why I'm ringing you," cut in Mrs. Johnson. "I'm not ringing to have a chat with you. I want you to warn your tart of a daughter to leave my son alone. My son is not going to marry the likes of her while I am alive. She can entice him as much as she wants. I know it is because of money. I will give her whatever she wants. Just ask her to leave him alone!"

Mrs. Beaton was dumbfounded at first. "Now,

hold on a minute, Madam," she managed to say at last, finding her voice. "How dare you call my daughter a tart? I am as worried about this marriage as you are. I don't like it any more than you do, but I care for my daughter's happiness."

"Her happiness? Is that all you can say? I'm not surprised. Good-for-nothing mother of a good-for-nothing child! You care for your daughter's happiness. Oh yes, you do. And you think my son is the one who will enrich your purse and make you both happy!"

"Madam," returned Mrs. Beaton, "I don't care about your money. What I have is enough for me. These children have made up their minds to go ahead with their plans. There's nothing any of us can do about it, whether we like it or not. Opposition will only make them more determined."

"Hmph, listen to this woman! I'm not surprised. I was sure you were no good as a mother yourself. No wonder Tolu speaks well of you. You've been aiding and abetting the whole thing all along, I'm sure." Mrs. Johnson spoke furiously and rapidly, not pausing for breath. "But never mind! We won't leave a kobo for him if he ever marries your daughter. You can go on encouraging them. Let me warn you that I shall show you who I am in this Lagos. And mark my words, your daughter shall regret marrying Tolu, if ever she does, and that will be over my dead body!" Thereafter, a torrent of solid abuse started pouring on poor Mrs. Beaton, who kept quiet for her daughter's sake.

When Mrs. Johnson at last paused for breath, Mrs. Beaton said, "I've got work to do, if you don't mind, Madam. You've shown me the sort of woman you are. I'm sorry for your son. If I had my way, Tokoni wouldn't marry into your family if Tolu were the last man on earth." She dropped the phone before Mrs. Johnson could get another word in. It rang again, but she ignored it. Mrs. Beaton stood there by the phone, her body trembling with rage. "What a malicious woman!" she said silently. "I wonder who she thinks she is? A sensible woman could not even speak to her housemaid the way she spoke to me!"

"Why aren't you answering the phone, Mummy? Shall I answer it?" demanded Elaye, zipping up her new dress as she came into the sitting room.

"No!" snapped her mother, then seeing the surprise on her daughter's face, she added gently, "Please, leave it."

"But why, Mummy? Who were you talking to? I heard you speaking so loudly, and you do look angry."

Mrs. Beaton looked at her daughter and bit her lower lip. She did not want to cry in front of Elaye, but she felt so humiliated and shaken that the tears could well fall any minute. She took a deep breath and told Elaye what happened.

"How dare she? And who is she herself? 'Show you who she is in this Lagos' indeed! Who knows her in Lagos? Anybody would think we have no money of our own. She probably thinks they are Da Rochas or some millionaires," Elaye fumed. "And calling Toks names! What did you say to her, Mummy?"

"What could I say? I only told..."

Elaye did not even let her mother finish. "Oh, Mummy!" she exploded, "what could you not have said? I thought as much! You let her be nasty to you and get away with it. There are a thousand and one things you could have said to her. She was lucky she didn't get me on the phone."

The phone started ringing again.

"Don't answer it, Elaye. It's her!" Mrs. Beaton knew instinctively it was Mrs. Johnson on the line.

"I won't let her go scot-free, Mummy. Let me answer that phone. Nobody talks rubbish to my mother and calls my sister names and gets away with it. I'll tell her what I think about her. She'll never be rude on the phone again in her life, never!" Elaye bristled, making for the phone.

"I said no, Elaye. Don't do that!" Her mother stopped her. "Tokoni will be hurt. And don't say anything about this to her. Leave it to me."

Elaye looked at her mother and shrugged, obviously annoyed that she could not tell Mrs. Johnson what she thought of her. "Well, isn't she lucky? I would have given her a nice slice of my tongue. Honestly, I don't know how you can be so soft. It beats me how you can take such humiliation from anybody and remain so calm."

"When you are a mother, you'll know. Then you'll understand what I'm talking about. I said leave this to me," her mother replied.

"Anyway, that's why we all love you. I must go now," Elaye continued, glancing at her watch. "I shall come home late this evening, so don't wait up for me. Bolou and I are going to a party."

"Won't you eat before you go?" her mother asked her. "It's foofoo and Egusi soup, your favorite."

"Hmm, too heavy." Elaye shook her head, laughed, kissed, and hugged her mother for being so thoughtful and ran out of the house.

Her mother watched her go and smiled to herself. Elaye was always in a hurry. What a contrast she was. Elaye and her only son Pere were not at all like Tokoni. Even as a baby, Elaye was fat and troublesome. She was a live wire but very jolly. Marie, who had wanted a boy for her second child, had not minded at all when she saw her baby, with the chubby face and head full of hair. Elaye had been born two years after Tokoni, who was a beautiful, tiny replica of her mother.

Tokoni was born only three days before her parents' first wedding anniversary. Everybody except Stephen's parents, who had wanted a boy for their son's first child, was so pleased about the baby. Marie, the only girl among seven children, had

wanted a girl and was overjoyed when Tokoni
came.

Tokoni was Marie all over again. She hated
scenes and avoided quarrels as much as she could.
When things got difficult, she preferred to
withdraw, even to hide and bear her sorrows
secretly. But the younger two were hot-tempered.
They took no insults from any quarters, and because
they were a close-knit family, they were ready to
fight for their quiet mother and elder sister. Elaye
could use her tongue just as fiercely as Pere could
use his fists. Their mother was glad they both dated
Ijaws. She had enough worries about Tokoni on her
mind without adding theirs. Her children had been
brought up and surrounded with so much love in
this family. They basked in this love and did not
know what the word hatred really meant. The
thought of her lovely, kind, young daughter going
defenseless into a family where she was disliked,
despised, even hated, was too much for her, and she
nearly wept.

She smiled wryly at Mrs. Johnson's accusations
that Tokoni was marrying her son for money and
that she was encouraging them. Money! What
would she want with other people's money? She had
not married a rich man. Stephen had been lucky to
get work at the General Hospital and earn a good
salary. But they had not had much money to spare
because he came from a poor family and was
helping to educate his younger brothers. Yet she
had not minded. What they had lacked in money
they had made up in love and happiness.

Money was nothing new to her. She had seen so much money as a little child and when she was young, her father being a chief and a Member of Parliament. Even now, her father was still a very rich and influential man, and all her brothers were highly placed in society. Money, she reflected now, if only Mrs. Johnson knew, has never been and will never be, please God, a problem to me.

She finished her cooking but could not eat. All she could think of was Mrs. Johnson's threats. Not that she believed there was anything in them, but they brought confirmation about the sort of problems her daughter would face in the Johnsons' household. It can be bad enough when other relatives are hostile to you, but actually to have the mother hate you so much would be unbearable. She felt even more protective towards Tokoni. She had had a good mother-in-law. The only time her mother-in-law was cold to her was when she had had a girl as her second baby, but as soon as a son came along, the dear soul was happy again and treated her like a daughter. She knew her sisters-in-law got on so well with her own mother. Her parents usually never interfered in their children's marital affairs except when they were asked for advice. So she had no firsthand experience of a truly divided household. She had merely gathered from other people's experiences that there was little happiness in such situations.

She prayed aloud for Tokoni all alone. "Good Lord, please help Tokoni. Show her where her happiness lies and don't forsake us, O Lord. We put our trust in Thee. Don't put us to shame."

She felt better for this and managed to swallow her lunch. Then she went to see her niece Bindo, who had just had a baby boy. Bindo was ill, so she took full control of Bindo's chores, and as she helped her, her mind was taken off Tokoni's problems.

Tokoni arrived home that evening, feeling on top of the world, and was disappointed to find only Pere at home. Pere was always either out at the Stadium or with his nose buried in a book. He had little time for girlish talk. Tokoni wished Elaye or her mother had been at home. *Trust my luck!* she thought. They both had to go out today of all days. She felt she had better tell somebody or burst with the weight of carrying her happiness.

Pere knew, as soon as he saw her, that something was afoot. She had tell-tale eyes, which betrayed her innermost feelings. He knew he was expected to listen, so he asked, "What's up, sis? You look as if you've won the pools or something."

"Pools ke? No o! Oh Pere, I'm so happy. Tolu's parents have invited me to their house this evening." Tokoni said excitedly, clapping her hands together like a little girl.

"Is that all?" Pere asked, amazed. "And what's so special about that? I would have thought that it was something more than that."

"But you don't understand, Pere," Tokoni said patiently. "It means they are coming to accept me as somebody to reckon with at last."

"I suppose so. But if I were Tolu, I wouldn't miss the opportunity of marrying a girl like you for all the world, my sis," Pere stated.

Tokoni laughed, and Pere laughed too. He enjoyed calling her "sis" or "my sis," and he knew she liked it. He never had any trouble with Tokoni. Elaye was always quarreling with him about something or other, but he loved her very much too. They got on like a house on fire despite their quarrels, and they always made up as soon as they finished arguing.

"Do you know, my sis," he added. "For someone like you, I could eat beans for two whole days!"

"Thank you, flatterer. I know you can never do that for anyone. You aren't that romantic," laughed Tokoni. It was a standing joke in their house. He had gone to spend his holidays, when he was in secondary school, with his father's sister and her family. This auntie had got the idea that beans were the best and cheapest nourishment for children. So she cooked them every day. When Pere came back home, he told his mother and sisters that he should never again be served beans.

They were so engrossed in their talk that they did not hear their mother come in until she closed the sitting-room door.

"Ah, welcome, Mummy," they greeted her.

"And where have you been? I'm starving!" came from Pere.

"Hello," their mother said, sitting down by Pere. "Lazybones, don't tell me you are so lazy that you can't even make your own supper."

"Ah, don't you know I'm a boy!" Pere demanded, his tongue in his cheek.

"And who said a boy is not meant to cook?" his mother countered, laughing. "I went to see Bindo. She is having a tough time, looking after that baby all alone and the house too. Right now she's ill. None of you have been to see her since she came home from hospital. She would appreciate your visits, even if you don't do any work for her, you know?" she added.

"I didn't know she was ill. How's the baby? We'll all go and see her on Sunday," said Tokoni.

"But I have a date on Sunday," Pere protested.

"You can go to your date from there, Oga. Don't be a spoilsport," replied his sister.

"Okay, but tell Elaye beforehand. I'd better change and start preparing the meal," their mother said, getting up.

"Oh no, you are not, Mummy," said Tokoni, pushing her gently back onto the chair. "I'm sure you've been helping sister Bindo all day. Now, let somebody else do the work for a change."

"What? No, o! Mummy, don't let her do it o!

Just go and cook yourself, please. She is too excited to do anything now. Can't see it written all over her face? I don't want to eat your burnt or tasteless food o," Pere cried in protest.

Tokoni shook her head, saying, "Don't mind him, Mummy. This son of yours is a joker. You wait, I'll tell you after supper. It's a surprise."

Pere laughed and said, "Hen hen!" teasing her as she went out of the room.

"Mummy, you've already made the foofoo," Tokoni called to her mother from the kitchen.

"Yes. Just warm up the soup."

Tokoni did that and brought the food to the table, and they all ate. She then told her mother of Mrs. Johnson's invitation. Mrs. Beaton was puzzled. *How odd,* she thought.

"How did you get this invitation?"

"She rang me up in the office this afternoon," the young girl replied, suspecting nothing.

"How did she sound? I mean, what did she say?" her mother asked again.

"Well, she sounded a bit cool, but that's her way to me. She has hardly spoken to me directly before. She said we should have a little chat and get to know each other."

"I wonder what that woman is up to," Mrs. Beaton said thoughtfully. "I don't understand why she should be inviting you today of all days. Do you know if Tolu will be at home tonight? I mean, will he be around?"

"Hmm, come to think of it, Mummy, I don't think he will. He's going to a Bachelor's Eve party tonight with his friends. Why all these questions? Why are you so worried?" Every instinct in her told her something was terribly wrong somewhere. She knew her mother had unpleasant news for her. She stared at her with big, round, frightened eyes.

Her mother took a deep breath and said, "I don't trust that woman! I don't want to worry you or upset you unnecessarily, my dear, but I wouldn't go if I were you. I know you are wondering why I say so. You see, Mrs. Johnson rang me up today. I suppose she got our number from the directory. She was very nasty. She said a lot of things I wouldn't want to repeat to you. It was horrible. So you see, Tokoni, I don't think she intends to be pleasant when you go there."

Tokoni had been staring at her mother, shocked and astonished, while she talked. She felt so sad that, instead of bringing her mother joy, she was only bringing her worry and unhappiness.

"Oh, Mummy, I'm so sorry. It must have been humiliating for you. I'm so sorry that instead of being a pride and joy to you, I'm causing you so much pain. I don't know how to beg for your forgiveness."

Her mother pulled her up and held her, like a little girl, in her arms. "Don't say that, Tokoni.

There's nothing to forgive. Never think that I'm ashamed of you. I'm not. I'm very proud of you, and all three of you are my joy. I don't know how I'd have managed without my children, especially you, Tokoni. You've been my inspiration all these years. You've helped me to go on. Yes, I'm worried about you, but I'm proud of you, and I love you very much. Never doubt that."

"I can't begin to thank you enough..." began Tokoni. Her mother put a finger on her lips before she could go on. "Stop thanking me," she scolded. "I'm only doing what a mother would do. Are you still going?"

"Do you think I should go?"

Her mother took another deep breath before saying gently, "I wouldn't like to stop you if you really want to go. It might be she has changed her mind. People have been known to change their minds in seconds, not to talk of hours. And on the other hand, she might be nasty. You have to give her the benefit of the doubt, if you want to go."

"I'm not going," Tokoni stated emphatically, then added as the phone began to ring, "This phone will never stop ringing!" She picked up the receiver.

"Tolu! I thought you'd be at your party tonight. Didn't you go?"

"Yes, I'm phoning from Soji's house. I wanted to tell you not to go to our house tonight," he explained. "I don't think you could be so silly as to believe my mother meant well. Couldn't you see

49

that if she did, she would have told me, and I'd be the one to tell you?"

"I don't know. I was probably thinking you knew and wanted to surprise me. Anyway, I've decided not to come any more."

"I'm so sorry. You see, I was just coming out of my room when I heard her talking to my aunt on the phone. She said she had invited you round and that she was going to tell the history of your forefathers. I waited until she dropped the phone, and then I confronted her. She said I had no right to listen to her conversation. Anyway, as usual, there was a terrible row, and in her anger, she told me about that call to your mother. Toks, I'm very sorry about it. I didn't know she could be so hard."

"I suppose it's because she is upset. You are their only son, and they are hurt. You know this is far from all their expectations. All their dreams about the traditional engagement and all that have gone to the dogs. And then they know there'll probably be many more disappointments for them in the future if you marry me. Don't blame them too much," Tokoni said soothingly.

"They'll just have to accept my choice. After all, it's not as if you can't speak Yoruba."

"It's different," Tokoni said, unwittingly using her mother's arguments. "But, Tolu, don't you think we'd better call the engagement off for now and wait some time? Perhaps we should give them a chance to get used to the idea. I feel in a way guilty for the way you and your parents have become enemies."

"No!" Tolu said fiercely. "I don't care if they never speak to me again, but I do care very much if you leave me. Please don't give up on me because of that, Tokoni. Don't ever leave me. I can't begin to imagine life without you. Don't blame yourself at all. You can't help it if they choose to be so unreasonable. Is that okay?"

"Okay!" Tokoni answered, laughing at the intensity with which he delivered his words one by one.

He laughed too and said, "That's better. Can I speak to your mother, if she is there? I'd like to apologize. It's such a shame."

"Hold on for her then. Bye till tomorrow." Tokoni turned to her mother. "He wants to speak to you, Mummy."

Marie Beaton, who had been watching and listening silently, got up and took the receiver. "Hello, Tolu," she said.

"How are you?"

"I'm fine, thank you, Ma. I don't know how to say this, but I'm very, very sorry. Honestly, I am. I want you to know that my mother's not all that bad. She doesn't know what she is doing. It's because she loves me. And she has a fiery temper and can say all sorts of things when she's angry, but she never means half of them. Please, forgive her," Tolu pleaded and paused for a moment. "I shouldn't expect you to understand. I can only say I'm sorry, and I beg you on her behalf. You don't know how ashamed of her I am..."

"Hush!" broke in Marie Beaton. "Never be ashamed of your mother. Of course, I understand. I am a mother too, you know. It's all right. I'm only worried for Tokoni, to tell you the truth. She is going to have a tough time if you marry her, with your mother feeling this way about her. It's all right, my dear. I'm not annoyed."

Tolu was grateful. "Oh, Mrs. Beaton, thank you very much. I assure you everything will be all right soon. Thank you and bye for now."

"Bye," said Mrs. Beaton and dropped the phone. Then she smiled at her daughter. Tokoni ran into her mother's arms and hugged her happily. They both started laughing, much to the surprise of Pere, who had just joined them. He had heard part of the conversation, and he did not think it was funny at all.

Tolu was relieved that Mrs. Beaton was so nice and understanding. He sat in a corner at Soji's party, looking so morose and thoughtful that Akinola, his best friend, couldn't help noticing there was something wrong. It was most unlike him because normally, he enjoyed these stag nights as much as every one of them. It was an unquestionable rule in their circle of friends that no girlfriends or wives tagged along. They always had the whole night to themselves and their man-to-man talks and habits.

Akin, as a rule, never interfered in other people's business.

But he knew at once that Tolu was thinking about Tokoni.

He liked Toks too. She was a great girl, and he couldn't understand why Tolu's parents should be so hostile and arrogant, but he knew at once that Tolu was thinking about Tokoni. He knew Tolu couldn't find a better girl. He also knew his own parents too would prefer him not to marry from another tribe. But he was sure that even if he brought home a white girl today as his future wife, they would give her a chance. They cared more about personality than the tribe or nationality. They were very understanding and rarely interfered in his private life.

"Funny this world!" he thought. "Here am I. My parents don't really care what tribe my wife comes from, so, of course, my girlfriend is Yoruba. And there's Tolu. His parents will only accept a Yoruba, so, of course, he had to go and fall in love with someone different. It's a pity we can't swap parents. How ironical the whole situation is."

"Mind if I share your thoughts?" he said jovially, but Tolu just stared straight ahead.

"This is serious," Akin said to himself. He pulled a chair up in front of Tolu and sat expectantly opposite him.

Tolu didn't know where to begin, but Akin coaxed him until the whole story came out. His blood went cold as he remembered the scene at home. He had come out of his room and had heard his mother talking to his Auntie 'Lape on the phone. He had just been in time to catch the last few words. He had no intention of eavesdropping, but his mother's words stopped him dead in his tracks.

"I've invited the brat here. I'll tell her a few home truths. I'll tell her the history of her kobokobo forefathers. Oh no! Tolu's joking too. He is not going to marry her while his father and I are alive. I'll see you tomorrow, Sister 'Lape. Say me well to Brother Femi and the children."

Tolu couldn't believe his ears. Auntie 'Lape was his mother's only sister and her chief adviser. Auntie 'Lape had never had much use for anyone who wasn't Yoruba and declared openly at all times that she was against intertribal marriages. She was lucky that all her five children had got married Yorubas. A strong-willed, stern, and formidable woman, she loved organizing other people's lives. She took nearly all the decisions in everything her younger brothers and sister did and took delight in mothering them. Tolu knew she must have filled his mother with fresh warnings on the bad traits in 'kobokobo,' especially their wickedness and disrespect for elders, which she never tired of harping on!

"Who's the brat, Mama?" he had asked his mother, going up to her. "Why are you inviting her?"

His mother looked completely taken aback.

"You were listening," she had accused him. "You're already learning their sly ways. It is your precious Tokoni. And when she comes here, I'll tell her a thing or two. I've already told her mother what I think of her. I called her this afternoon." She couldn't stop herself once she started, and she went on and on. They were only after Tolu's money, she had said, and they were not going to get it. That had made Tolu laugh, and he had told her they had more than their own share of wealth.

"Do you think you are the only rich people around?" he had asked her angrily. "They don't show off like you do, and they don't go to society parties, but that does not make them poor. And what's money anyway? The love and understanding in their house makes them ten times richer than you."

Just at that moment, his father came in. He had been having a short nap, and their raised voices had disturbed his sleep. He had heard part of the row and felt his presence was needed. He sat down on the revolving armchair and said, "Tolulope, for all I know, marry that girl and I'm finished with you. And I mean that."

He said this in that voice that used to make Tolu tremble, the voice that said, "This is my final word!" and with this, he revolved the chair so that his back was turned to them. But this time, it did not cut any ice with Tolu. It annoyed him to see his father treating him like a child. Did they know he was a grown man now?

"Look, Papa," he flared. "I don't care. I don't need your consent to get married, neither do I need your money. What do I lose if you finish with me? I've got my job, and thank God, it's a paying job, so my dear father, you can leave your money to whoever you like. I don't need it."

"That girl and her mother must have used some 'kobokobo' charms to bewitch you. If not, I see no reason why you should be so obstinate. After all, she is not the most beautiful girl in this Lagos. And not only one road leads to Oyo, ke," his mother said.

"Yes," Tolu retorted, with a touch of sarcasm, "they have bewitched me with love, Mama, with love, kindness, laughter, and all the qualities that make their family. Theirs is by far a better family than ours. And Mrs. Beaton, though she is both mother and father to her children, is doing a very good job of it. Tokoni may not be the most beautiful girl in Lagos to you, but then, you don't see what I see in her. To me, she is the most beautiful of women. There are many roads leading to Oyo indeed, but all travelers pass by the road of their choice."

"You don't know what you are talking about..." began his mother.

"I haven't finished," Tolu interrupted her. "You'll be surprised to see that I know what I'm doing. You had no time for me as a child. I did not come to you with my problems. Why don't you leave me to lead my life as I like it now?"

"That's not true, you ungrateful son! We did all we could for you. You had the best of everything money could buy!" his father exploded, getting up from the chair for the first time since the row began.

Tolu had walked out on them. He knew he was being very rude, but it could not be helped. If he had stayed on in that room for another couple of minutes, he would have been forced to say some very unforgivable things.

"Honestly, Akin," he said, "when I was a boy, they had little time for me. All they did was to shower me with presents and show me off to their friends because I was very brilliant." Tolu's thoughts went back to his childhood. His parents had been too busy with their own social life, running their business, entertaining their friends, and holding parties to have much time for him. He had had lots of clothes, toys, and books—anything, in fact, that money could buy. These material things, however, gave him little comfort.

He spoke again. "I was closer to my granny than to either of them. It was my granny who bathed and fed me and treated all my cuts and bruises. She was the one who shared my childish secrets and solved all my childish problems. Now I am a man, and they want to run my life."

Akin didn't say anything. He knew Tolu needed to talk about these things. He knew Tolu's grandmother. She was a good soul and now lived in Abeokuta with her eldest son and his family.

"I was sent to the best boarding school in Ibadan even before I was nine. And all through Secondary School, the boarding house was my first home and my own home the second," Tolu went on. "I was more at ease with friends than I was with my parents because I had grown up too much away from them."

His parents, Tolu reflected, had always been genuinely happy to have him at home during the holidays, but they did not visit him as much as he would have liked at school. He had been happy at first because he had more toys, books, clothes, and money than his friends. He had mistaken material things for love and companionship. It was only when he was in his teens, at the Igbobi College, that he had realized that he needed more than their lavish presents and rare visits. He knew that in their way, they loved him and were very proud of his achievements. They were not friends. There was no sympathy and understanding between them. He had needed their love, time, and understanding more than he ever needed their presents.

"I have promised myself that my children will never go to the boarding house unless it is what they really want to do. I will always follow their growth, achievements, and activities with real interest. We will be friends as well as a family."

Akin listened to his friend and felt really sorry for him. It wasn't much fun being in love, he decided. There were too many problems, one way or the other. If it was not the girl's parents, it was the boy's, or the girl didn't love the boy as much as he loved her, or vice versa. At twenty-seven, he ought to have married or at least gotten engaged to someone now, by the standards of his circle of friends. But not Akin. He had not found the girl he could give up his freedom for. His present girlfriend, Lolade, had been on and off with him for a year now, but he still didn't feel he couldn't live without her. He liked her very much; sometimes he even felt he loved her, but not enough to marry her yet. Tolu's voice brought his thoughts to an abrupt stop.

"I always wonder why they want me to do things their way, now that I am older. Especially my father. What they don't realize is that I am like him. I have that stubborn streak in me too. If I want something very much, I make sure I get it." Here was something that involved his happiness, his whole life, and he was going to get it, he declared silently.

"You really have this thing bad, old boy." Akin tried to make a joke of the situation.

Tolu gave a wry smile and nodded.

"All I can tell you," Akin went on, "is to follow the dictates of your heart and your head. Do what you want, but make sure it's what is best. Don't try to please anybody. If they can't beat you, they'll join you in the end. I'm sure if they knew Toks better, they wouldn't object so much. So, old boy, let true love take its course. You can't find a better girl, I'll tell you that."

"That's right, Akin," Tolu replied. "Who was it that said, 'There is only one good reason for marriage—when two people love each other'?" he wondered. That person knew what he was talking about. There was no way he, Tolulope Johnson, would not go on and marry Tokoni Beaton, when they both loved each other so much.

"Come on then, cheer up. You are a man!" he heard Akin say. "Who's going to cheer Toks up if you are like this yourself? You should learn to take your troubles in your stride."

"Sure. You are right again, Akin," Tolu agreed, grateful for Akin's advice. He was soon into the party, laughing and joking around, as if he had no cares in the world.

CHAPTER FOUR

Tokoni sat in the car and thought about life with Tolu for the past nine weeks. She wouldn't have believed that he could change so much. He had become very irritable and moody, always looking tired and easily annoyed. He, who had always been over-punctual for their dates, now skipped almost every one or came late. This particular night, he had been late for their dinner date. She had waited for almost an hour before he came, all moody and worn out. He had apologized for being late, but Tokoni couldn't get it out of her mind. They had planned to go to the new Chinese Restaurant along Ikorodu Road, and she knew he would love the food because he liked Chinese and Indian food, and so did she.

Tokoni was dressed in a pale pink cotton dress that was elegantly cut, drawn into pleats down the sides of the waist, and plain in the front and the back. She had just bought this dress, and this was the first time she ever wore it. She knew it suited her very well, and she had hoped the brightness and elegance would appeal to Tolu, whatever mood he was in tonight. He didn't even notice. It was unlike him, but he said nothing about the dress. He had always been alert to her way of dressing and always paid her compliments. He never failed to tell her when a dress suited her or not and had always noticed if it was new.

They had not said much on the drive to the Restaurant. And during the meal, which was served in three courses, she had noticed that he was merely toying with the Sweet and Sour Pork, a dish which had always been a great favorite of his. But when she asked him what the matter was, he shook his head and said nothing. She persisted, and he snapped at her to mind her business and eat her own food.

Tokoni was surprised. She couldn't understand why Tolu was so beastly these days. She couldn't bear this. So far as she was concerned, the situation had deteriorated. She constantly found her emotions at war with the dictates of her conscience over the situation in Tolu's house. She could no longer pretend not to see the feelings of resentment Tolu sometimes had for her. She wondered if he might not be having second thoughts about the whole thing. She hadn't been able to resign herself to the fact that he was yielding under all the pressure at home. She realized now the day of reckoning was nearer than she had thought. She had been half-expecting it, but when it finally did happen, she couldn't believe it. She would have found it more bearable had Tolu told her it was all over. This suspense, not knowing what would happen, was killing her. She felt she must get it out now or never.

"Tolu," she began, "I can't understand your behavior these days. You seem as if you are just humoring me by taking me out. Don't you love me anymore? Would you rather we call it quits here? Personally, I think a total break would be better than the way we have been going on."

"Have you finished?" Tolu asked, scowling. "You like reading meanings into everything one does. It's to avoid this sort of situation that I came out with you at all, if you must know. Look, stop nagging me. I get more than enough of that at home without you adding yours. God knows, I've had more than my own fair share these past few weeks. And if this is the way this evening is going to be, we'd better go home."

On the way, they were both silent, concentrating on their own thoughts. Tolu was battling with his conscience. One voice kept saying, "You are being very cruel. Don't treat her like this. You know it's not her fault. She's having a rough time too. She's suffering with you. Try to make it easier for her. You love her more than anything, and she loves you, so why hurt her?" The other said, "Leave her. She has her fair share of being petted. Let her say she is sorry this time. You are the one always apologizing. What did you do? You deserve a lecture from her?"

These thoughts kept flashing over Tolu's mind, warring with each other. It was as if they were tearing him apart.

He stopped abruptly at her gate. He hadn't realized they had gotten that far.

"Goodnight," Tokoni said quietly, about to

open the door. Her gentle voice and lovely sad face melted Tolu's heart, and he caught hold of both her hands and took them in his. All his resolves to be hard with her were forgotten.

"Toks," he said.

"Yes?" she answered, her eyes turned away from him.

"Toks, love, look at me, please," Tolu pleaded. "I'm sorry. I don't know what came over me. I suppose it's the strain. But I love you, try to understand that. I love you very much, and your happiness is my concern. Please forgive me."

"Oh Tolu, I couldn't bear it if we started quarreling. I know you are very, very tired of it all. So am I. I love you, too, but I doubt if I can stand much more. Now let's forget it and go home. You need some sleep. I can see you are tired. I am, too. Goodnight."

"Goodnight and sweet dreams," replied Tolu, kissing the tips of her fingers.

She climbed out of the car and said, "See you on Friday." Tolu waited in the car, saw her go through the gate and down the lawn to their front door. She turned and waved to him before letting herself in. He drove off, little dreaming that this night might have marked a turning point. Things had drifted on long enough. As far as Tokoni was concerned, the time had come for a change!

As she undressed in her room, Tokoni allowed

her mind to wander to a couple of irritating incidents. These had brought home some of her mother's doubts about marriage working between them, regardless of traditional differences. Tolu had come to their house and had met Ebitimi there, playing cards with Pere. Everyone had been talking in Ijaw as he came in. Of course, they switched languages straight away, but still, he looked as if he wondered what they had been saying. Ebitimi had greeted Tolu warmly, even though he knew this was the guy who held the key to the heart of the girl he felt was the only one for him. They had all sat down and talked together, both Tokoni and Tolu watching the other two play their game of Whot until Elaye came in with her boyfriend, Bolou, both declaring that they were starving.

"What sort of soup did Mummy cook today?" Elaye asked.

"Banga," Tokoni replied.

"With fresh fish, and it does taste nice! I was just in time for lunch, and we had it with starch," Ebitimi informed Elaye and Bolou.

"That's right, Banga soup tastes better with starch than anything else," Bolou agreed.

"What sort of soup is Banga soup, and how on earth do you people eat starch?" Tolu demanded. Even to his own ears, the phrase "you people" sounded abrupt.

"Banga is palm fruit. We cook Banga soup by cooking the ripe palm fruits and extracting the oil from them. Then we use it to cook with instead of the usual palm oil. It tastes delicious," Tokoni explained.

"I suppose it will, but how can you eat starch? Or isn't it the same starch we put in clothes?" Tolu asked again in a sharp voice.

"Yes, it is, but we mix it with cold water and cook it with palm oil, and it tastes delicious. How come you've never tried it?" Elaye remarked. "You've been here often enough."

"I'll never eat that stuff!" Tolu said indignantly.

"Don't be so superior, Tolu," Tokoni said. "I'll make it for you, and you will enjoy it, I assure you."

"Oh no, you won't. I won't have that thing cooked in my house when we are married," Tolu maintained.

"Oh, come off it, old boy. It's far, far better than that messy black stuff you call *amala*," Pere observed, joining in the conversation which was becoming heated.

"Of course, it's not. Amala is such a nourishing food..." began Tolu.

"So is starch," Bolou cut in.

"It's enough. Let's put a stop to this conversation before it turns into a row. We come from different backgrounds, and as they say, 'One man's meat is another man's poison,'" Ebitimi remarked good-humoredly.

"Yes. Just like you can't stand the thought of starch, most of us can't stand amala, but we eat it all the same," Tokoni couldn't help adding.

"So there's no need for you to turn up your nose at our food," Elaye added for good measure. The phrase "our food" sounded abrupt too.

Then as best as he could, Ebitimi had changed the conversation to other subjects. It was only a few minutes later when Tolu announced that he must be going that Tokoni realized he had been unusually silent. He had talked only when someone spoke to him. She got up and straightened the folds of her dress as he said his goodbyes.

"Don't kiss at the gate, o! Love is blind, they say, but remember the neighbors aren't," Ebitimi advised with his characteristic good humor.

"We'll remember that," Tokoni laughed as she went out of the sitting room with Tolu. She smiled again as she closed the door behind her.

"Is that tender smile for me or Ebitimi?" Tolu's deep voice broke into her thoughts, and she answered him at random.

"He is such a funny man. Imagine coming up with something like that."

Tolu glanced down at her mockingly. "He appears to be more your kind of man—rich, amusing, and handsome. There would be no barriers if you two decided to get married to each other," he remarked with satire. "You could chat and laugh all the time over your starch and *Banga* soup."

Tokoni bit her lip and sent a silent prayer to heaven for serenity. She knew they were on slippery ground, and she had only to give him back as good as he gave her to turn this into another of those rows they were always having these days. Whatever happened, she must keep calm.

"Goodnight, Tolu," she said coolly.

"Till when?" he asked.

"Any time. You know I'm nearly always in," she replied. "I'll see you tomorrow. Goodnight."

Tokoni waited until his car was out of sight before walking thoughtfully into her house, but she couldn't join in the fun the others were having. Tolu had spoiled the day for her. She guessed he was piqued because she had not taken his side in the argument about starch versus *amala.* But how could she have done so when all her life she had been eating and enjoying starch? They hardly ever ate amala at home. Her mother only prepared it occasionally, but they ate starch at least twice a month. And she couldn't begin to throw aside all her own customs, deny herself delicious local food just because she was engaged to be married to a Yoruba man. After all, you don't go agreeing with everything your fiancé says, even if you know he isn't right, just because he says so. What a topic to disagree about!

That was only one occasion. The other one was another argument on an old but still very widely

practiced Ijaw custom, **excision**. It was Ebitimi
again who unwittingly caused this, a few days after
the starch-amala episode. Tolu had come to their
house and had met Ebitimi there again, playing
Whot with Pere. Again, he received a warm
welcome and was invited to join in the game, but he
declined politely. Then Ebitimi had asked Tokoni if
she would be excised.

"Of course, and with the traditional pomp too,"
Tokoni had replied in a matter-of-fact way.

"What does an educated girl like you want to
go and do such a thing for?" Tolu demanded,
offended that Ebitimi should speak about such an
intimate topic.

"It's our custom. Mummy will be heartbroken if
I don't do it."

"I think it's a primitive custom and rather
dangerous too. You would lose a lot of blood, if you
don't know. You could get an infection from the
wound," Tolu said.

"So I keep telling them, but no one listens to
me. I tell them the human body has just enough
blood to manage on. During the process of excision,
you could lose so much that what remains won't be
enough for you," Pere supported him. "Then there's
the risk of infection too. Honestly, it's a very
unhealthy custom."

"What I don't understand is why your Dad,
being a doctor himself, didn't insist on having it
done when you were babies. That's the way a lot of

my cousins and a great number of people I know do theirs these days," Ebitimi remarked.

"Probably because he was a doctor. You know this custom is very much out of favor with hospitals," Tolu said.

"I know, but the people who perform the rite out of hospitals are midwives and doctors, if you don't know," Tokoni told him.

"Still, it's such a barbaric custom which should be scrapped, and those midwives and doctors..." began Tolu.

"No, it should not be. I heard that girls who don't do it are very amorous—nymphomaniacs to be exact," Ebitimi joked, trying to thaw the ice in the atmosphere.

"There's no truth in that assertion. It was only culled to justify a primitive custom. No educated person should indulge in it," Tolu said.

"It has nothing to do with education really, Tolu," Pere explained to his brother-in-law-to-be. "Our people believe that if a woman who is not excised has children, they should be treated as outcasts. They should have nothing to say in anything concerning our people."

"All these dangers you people are talking about don't scare me at all. I know over fifty people who have done this thing, and nothing of that sort happened to them," Tokoni declared.

"Well, it does not have to be immediate. It

could happen years and years later. They could have problems in the future, and it could be traced to the butchery they had years ago," Tolu said.

"Hear, oh hear!" Ebitimi joked.

"It's true, Ebitimi. You won't believe because there are no statistics to prove it to you. If someone had conducted a survey into the after-effects, then probably it would have meant something to you," Pere told Ebitimi.

"What is all this fuss about? I won't be the first to be excised, and I dare say the custom won't end with me. Nothing will happen to me, in the process or as a result of it," Tokoni maintained stubbornly.

"We are telling you all these for your own good," Tolu warned her.

"And anyway, since Tokoni is not marrying into the clan—is that the right word?—she might be exempted if you are so strongly opposed to it," Ebitimi offered, trying to console Tolu.

"Of course, I will do nothing of the sort," Tokoni declared stoutly. "I am going to be excised, and nobody is going to stop me."

"Oh well, I guess nobody can, and after that, I suppose it's the fattening room next," Tolu remarked.

"No, we don't have that as one of our customs, so I won't go through that," Tokoni had replied smoothly.

There was a devil in her that could spring to life when challenged so blatantly, she knew. She wasn't being deliberately disagreeable, but Tolu was a real pain in the neck these days. Once, they hadn't been able to look at each other without smiling. They had always been on the edge of laughter because most of their thoughts and likes coincided.

Now, all that was going. A sweet relationship was turning sour before its fulfillment, all because of these silly bickerings. Like her, he was unsettled when once her company had been all that he desired.

Tokoni sighed, sinking down onto the end of her bed. Did it really matter? Were all these soul-searchings really worth it? Could it be true that she and Tolu were unlikely to make it together? Her mother's arguments about Tolu not trying to understand her customs and language came back to her. He was just being superior for no reason, and it was only to be expected that things between them would grow oppressive with tension. She decided that she couldn't take any more, and if things didn't change, she would leave him.

But why was she examining her feelings tonight? she wondered. She knew the answer. In their little circle of friends, word had gotten around that Tolu was seeing quite a bit of one final-year student nurse. It hadn't worried Tokoni much before, but after the Restaurant episode, it had just come creeping into her mind. She knew that this girl, Doyin Akano, had lots of charm. It had been on her mind to ask him about her, but she realized that

he would only tell her what he wanted her to know.
And anyway, she had been quite sure this girl was
just a passing fling who meant nothing to Tolu. But
all the same, she had felt a bit threatened, especially
since the girl was Yoruba. Tolu probably felt
uncertain about Ebitimi. She knew in her heart that
he had nothing to fear on that score, but after
tonight's episode, she wasn't quite sure whether
things between them would be the bliss she had
imagined. What should she do?

The next day, she went to see her friend,
Nkechi. Tokoni had a lot of friends, but she
confided only in Nkechi. Ever since their school
days, they had shared their secrets and problems.
They had been friends for over seven years now,
and each was accepted as a member of the other's
family, even though Nkechi was Igbo and Tokoni
Ijaw. Nkechi, like all Tokoni's friends, knew and
liked Tolu. And lucky Nkechi, Tokoni thought, she
had no problems of this sort, as her boyfriend was
Igbo too.

Nkechi Nwabogu listened as Tokoni told her
about her problems and didn't know what to say.
Nkechi had never been much of an adviser. It was
Tokoni who knew about these things and what sort
of advice was needed for all sorts of problems. Not
surprisingly, when it came to her own case, she
didn't know what to do.

"How true the saying is, that a physician cannot
heal himself," Nkechi said to herself. "Imagine
Tokoni at a loss for advice." She knew Tokoni
loved Tolu, and Tolu loved her too, so one couldn't

advise her to break off with him. Poor Toks, she looked so sad. Nkechi felt like crying for her. She didn't know what advice to give. She didn't even know what to say to comfort her. They both sat there, lost in their respective thoughts.

"Yes, I've got it. I know what to do." Tokoni's voice cut through Nkechi's thoughts.

Nkechi, puzzled, looked at her.

"I'm going to break with Tolu," Tokoni explained. "I've just remembered that we need some secretaries in our new offices opening at Benin and Port Harcourt. I will apply and go there. I just hope they haven't got enough people yet. I'll talk to my boss anyway. I know he will help."

"Why go all the way to Port Harcourt to forget him? Why leave all your family and friends?"

"Oh, Nkechi, don't you know? It won't work if I stay here."

"He won't take no for an answer, and we'll only be getting at each other's throats if we continue like this. It's a break we both need. All this is because of the relationship he now has with his parents. It's the strain telling on him. I am not going to stand by and let them disown him. It will kill his spirit. He loves and needs them a lot."

"And what about you? What about him and your love? Do you think he will let you go?" Nkechi asked, not approving.

"I'm going to tell him I'm going away. I won't

tell him when or where I'll be going to."

"Is that fair?" Nkechi demanded.

"It's the only way. I'm fed up with things as they are. He already has a Yoruba girlfriend. When I go away, he will soon forget me and will marry her or someone they will approve of," Tokoni said calmly.

"How do you know that's what he will do? I think you should talk this over with him before taking any rash decisions," Nkechi protested.

"No. He'll try to stop me. The only talking over I will do with Tolu is to tell him I'm going away. Where or when will be a mystery to him."

"If I know Tolu, he'll come looking for you," Nkechi declared.

"So he will, but he won't be able to trace me. He will guess where I've gone, but I'll make sure as few people as possible know where I am. Even if Tolu wanted to look for me, he would be on his National Youth Service Corps then. He takes his work so seriously; you won't find him gallivanting round Port Harcourt looking for any estranged fiancée. He doesn't even know we are having a new office in Port Harcourt."

"All right. How long do you intend to be away for?" Nkechi demanded, shaken by this change of heart.

"I don't know yet. Probably as long as it takes him to forget me and get married," Tokoni replied.

"What happens after?"

"After he gets married? Well, I'm taking things one at a time. I won't look too much ahead into the future. But I'll probably get married too and stay on in Port Harcourt. Though if I do get married, it won't be for love. It would be for the companionship." Tokoni said.

"I think you are taking this too far. You know as well as I do..." Nkechi began.

"Nkechi," Tokoni cut in, "it's subject to change. If Tolu's attitude changes before the whole thing comes through, I'll gladly give this idea up. If not, I'll go ahead with it. Just promise me that you won't give him my address if I go or tell him about this discussion."

Nkechi sighed. "Well, I don't know that this is the best thing to do," she said uncertainly, "but I know you better than to try to stop you. If this is the way you want it, I promise you I'll not give you away."

Tokoni flashed Nkechi a grateful smile. "Thank you, dear. I know I can always rely on you. I shall miss Tolu so! I love him so very much, but we can't go on like this."

She was about to cry as she finished this sentence. She could feel the tears pushing at her eyelids, but she held them back by force before they could start trickling down her cheeks. "I shan't cry," she said to herself, "because I know I am doing the right thing for him." When she got home that evening, she told her family of her decision.

Elaye was furious. She minced no words in telling her elder sister what she thought of the whole thing. "But you can't do that, Toks! You'll die of a broken heart. Anyway, I know you won't forget Tolu, you'll see."

"Of course, my heart won't break or any such thing. I'll be very much alive and well too. And the aim of my going is for him to forget me, not vice versa. I don't want him to have to choose between me and his parents," Tokoni explained to them, her eyes pleading with her brother and sister to see it her way. They didn't seem convinced.

"That's for him to decide, not you, sis. You are not doing him any good by taking this decision alone. And when will you stop putting others first and think about yourself first?" asked Pere.

"Yes, when?" echoed Elaye. "But Pere, you are wrong. She has thought of herself first this time. Anyway, I'm sure Tolu won't forget you, quite sure. He'll come looking for you."

'I know what I'm doing,' Tokoni said stubbornly and went on to explain how Tolu would be on N.Y.S.C. then and wouldn't have the time to come looking for her as he wouldn't even know her address. Her brother and sister proceeded to give the same reasons as Nkechi gave for her decision being wrong and she had the same answers ready for all their arguments.

"And Mummy, you are not saying anything.

This is crazy! I'm sure you are in favor of this. Honestly, you both just drive me mad with your selfless love, giving, giving, giving all the time," Elaye said angrily.

Their mother had been listening quietly all along. She didn't really know what to say, but she felt if Tokoni and Tolu could forget each other during that period, it would be a good thing for all concerned. She hated herself for looking at it this way, but rather than let her daughter go into that house where she was hated so much, she would prefer her to forget Tolu. She knew it wasn't fair on him at all, yet there was no stopping Tokoni.

"My dear children, Tokoni is an adult. She has decided what she wants to do. She is only informing us now. What we say now will make no difference. Personally, I think it would be best."

"You would!" cut in Elaye sarcastically.

"I mean, everybody will have peace of mind," Marie continued, ignoring her daughter's remark, "if they could forget each other. That's not for me to say. It's not my business, it's theirs."

"I'm glad you know that," Elaye cut in rudely again.

Her mother ignored her once more and went on, "We can all only pray for her, that since this door seems closed, somehow the Lord should open another for her. I'm very proud of her, I dare say, for being the one to take this sort of decision. Considering what she feels about Tolu, this needs a lot of courage."

"Courage, my foot! This is not what is called courage. This is cowardice. Why doesn't she stay here and fight it out with his parents instead of taking the easy way out? It won't do any good, I tell you," Pere objected.

"Pere, please let me finish," his mother said. "We shall all miss Tokoni very much, but we won't all stay together forever. One time or another, we are bound to leave one another for someone or somewhere else. But we shall still be joined in heart and meet again from time."

"I suppose you are right there, Mummy. Well, Toks, all the best. So when is this transfer coming through?" Elaye asked.

"I don't know yet. I haven't even told them at the office, so I don't know if it will happen. I'll let you know tomorrow. But anyway, it all depends on Tolu. If his attitude changes, then whatever preparations I've made, I'll cancel them for him," Tokoni said with a sad smile.

"I hope they don't let you go. I will be very happy if they don't. I don't see any good in all this. I'm still saying it. Women! Anyway, all the best," Pere added grudgingly, and they all laughed.

Fortunately for Tokoni, her boss was very understanding. When she told him everything, he understood why she wanted to go and promised to help. He asked her to write an application there and then and personally processed it for her, making it as much of an official secret as possible.

While this was going on, Tokoni had another row with Tolu, which left her with no qualms about what she was doing. It was her mother's birthday, and Ebitimi had brought a gilt-framed mirror as a present. The mirror was such a lovely thing, and it had delighted Tokoni, who was all alone at home then, so much that she had impulsively flung her arms around his neck and reached up to kiss him. Ebitimi was stunned by her action. He had some idea of hanging on to her and kissed her again. Anyway, she found herself laughing. They both turned instinctively to see Tolu at the door way.

He greeted them coolly. "Am I interrupting something?"

"Of course not," Tokoni said with dignity. "I was just thanking Ebitimi for the lovely present he brought for Mummy." Her heart was hammering as she saw that he was not amused. She knew that a row was imminent.

Tolu and Ebitimi exchanged a few banal remarks, and then Ebitimi had gone. There was more than mere annoyance in Tolu's manner, and Ebitimi, she supposed, had guessed the atmosphere was full of ice once again.

"How long has Ebitimi been here?" Tolu asked in tones, distant and chilly.

"About fifteen minutes," Tokoni answered.

"Was that the end of a long greeting I

witnessed just now?" His voice was rough, and she noticed the tired lines around his eyes for the first time. He had always been so full of fun, and to see him like this, tired and dispirited, hurt like a physical pain.

"I already told you he came to give Mummy a birthday present. What...?"

"And what a lovely thank you he got from the grateful daughter. Lucky rich boy!" Tolu sneered.

"I wonder why you have gone so sour on Ebitimi. And I think you are just yearning for a row. I won't give you the satisfaction of having one, though."

"Ah, who is talking about a row? Every time I come here these days, the guy is around. You all get on so well with him, I don't know what else to think. We only have to argue about something, and you'll take his side. It's..."

"You are just being unreasonable. Why should you expect me to renounce all I believe in, when you crook your finger? Why should I not retain my identity just because you think differently?"

"I wonder what will happen with this Ebitimi guy when I go on Youth Service Corps. I wouldn't be surprised if..."

Tokoni gave a gasp of almost physical pain. "You have no need to worry your head about that. I shall be going away myself too, probably before you go on your Youth Service or just afterwards."

"Where are you going?" Tolu demanded.

"I don't intend to tell you where and when. I just want to get away from all these bickerings," Tokoni replied.

"Is that the only reason why you are going away? What about your work?"

"I could resign if I wanted. I just must get away."

"And how long will you be away for?"

"A year, two years, or more. I don't know."

"So what happens to us?" Tolu wanted to know.

"I don't know. If there is still an 'us' by then, I guess things will work out."

"What exactly are you getting at?" Tolu demanded, but he couldn't get a favorable answer from her. They had a row, with Tolu accusing her of not loving him anymore, and she, in turn, accusing him of the same thing. He went home that day, feeling really bad.

Very soon, Tokoni's transfer came through. She talked to her boss and told him she didn't want anyone except her own family to know her whereabouts. He understood the problem and promised not to reveal where she was, and she was all set to go. On the day she was leaving Lagos, they had been invited to a party, so she left a letter for Tolu with her mother and traveled on the second flight of the day.

Her family saw her off at the airport. Suddenly, Elaye started crying, and soon both Tokoni and their mother joined in too. This was the first time they were going to be separated, and heaven alone knew how long Tokoni was going to be away. They could and would visit her, but it would not be the same as all living together in their house, and they would miss her so much.

Tokoni got to Port Harcourt and was met at the airport by her grandparents. They were both very strong and healthy, especially her grandmother. They welcomed her warmly, and she felt quite at home in no time at all. She was glad she didn't have to share a room with anybody. She needed to be alone with her thoughts and her memories of the good times she had had with Tolu. Now she had thrown all that away, but it was in his best interest, she consoled herself. She went into her room after eating and wondered how Tolu would receive the letter. She lay on the bed thinking until he seemed to be there beside her. She could almost smell that faint, pleasant aroma of the aftershave he used. She smiled to herself as tears fell down her cheeks until she fell asleep, out of sheer fatigue.

CHAPTER FIVE

Tolu came eagerly to collect Tokoni for the party. This evening, he was in a good mood because his parents had been out, and he hadn't seen them or been nagged before coming. When he rang the bell at Tokoni's house, he wasn't at all prepared for the shock he received that night. It was answered by Mrs. Beaton. She greeted him with a smile, which he noticed was a bit strained, and invited him in. She offered him a drink, but he refused. Something told him all was not well here. He could see that Mrs.Beaton was sad. Her smile seemed forced, and her eyes were red and swollen as if she had been crying.

"Is Toks not ready?" he asked casually.

Mrs. Beaton walked to the television set and took a letter from the top. She gave it to Tolu and said, "She's not here. She left this for you."

"What do you mean, she is not here? Where is she?" Tolu asked frantically, taking the letter from Mrs. Beaton and sensing calamity.

"That letter will enlighten you better," Mrs. Beaton explained briefly and bit her lip.

Tolu stared at the envelope, wondering where Tokoni could be and why she should be writing to him. He quickly tore the envelope open and read the letter hurriedly.

Dear Tolu,

I am really very sorry I have to take this decision, but we've reached a turning point. I could not tell you I would be leaving today because I knew you would try to stop me, and I believe what I'm doing is for the best. Tolu, I love you very much, and through everything, my love for you has remained unshaken. It is this love that has kept me going all along. But now I am not of the opinion that marriage between you and me will be any good.

If you forsake your family for me now, some day in the future you might regret it and hate me for being the cause of your having no relations. I would hate that. I don't want to be a source of unhappiness to you. I don't want to hamper your life in any way. Don't I know what your father's money and family ties can do for you? Don't I know what you mean to your parents and what they mean to you? We are not yet married, but the strain of being constantly on the warpath with your parents is telling on you already. It has engulfed you so much that you are always moody and irritable. What then will happen when we are married?

I can stand indifference from your parents, but not from you, Tolu. These past weeks, I have been at the end of my tether. I have tried my best, God knows I have, but I can't stand it any longer. It's been such a strain for me, even more than it has been for you, knowing I am not accepted through no fault of mine. Yet I have continued being nice to them. Why can't they give me a chance? I don't know. I'm sure once I'm outside this Lagos, it will be easier for you to forget me.

So, Tolu, I'm leaving you. My love will always be with you. I hope you find happiness with someone else, the type of happiness we had before, and with someone your parents will approve of. Thank you for all the good times we had. I am glad I have those memories at least. I love you. Please don't try to look for me as I won't come back to you.

Take care. God bless you always.

All the love in my heart.

Tokoni

Tolulope Johnson could not believe his eyes. He read the letter quickly once more before the meaning finally sank into him. He couldn't believe that Tokoni had really left him. Why, he had seen her only a couple of days ago, and she didn't even give him a hint. He knew she had planned it well in advance. She seldom did things on impulse. Hadn't she told him before that she would probably leave before he went on his Youth Service or soon after?

"Why did she do this? Why did you allow her to go, and where has she gone? You can't tell me you don't know." He threw the questions one after the other at Tokoni's mother without waiting for an answer.

"Of course I know," said Mrs. Beaton slowly. "Do you expect me to deny it? But I can't tell you where she is. She made us all promise not to tell you, and I can't break that promise. I'm sorry, Tolu."

"Do you want to see me go mad with worry? I could face my parents because she was here with me, but now... I don't know how I'm going to manage. Please tell me where she is," Tolu begged.

"I am sorry, my dear, I can't tell you. It's her decision, and she thinks it's for the best. There was no way I could stop her. You know her too," Mrs. Beaton explained.

"So you mean she's gone for good, and you can't bring her back?" he asked Tokoni's mother quietly.

"I'm sorry, my dear, very sorry, but I can't bring her back. That just about sums it up," Mrs. Beaton said.

"Well, thank you, Ma, and bye-bye. But just one more thing. In another week, I'll be going to Sokoto for my N.Y.S.C. Before I go, I'll try my best to see whether I will be lucky to find someone who can help me. In case I fail, though, can I write to her through you?"

Mrs. Beaton didn't have the heart to refuse. She could see that this had hit Tolu very hard. He looked so distraught, and she felt sorry for him. "Really, she insisted on no communication with you, but if you want me to pass on any message to her, I will. Don't be so down-hearted. You'll soon feel better." She bade him farewell with a heavy heart. She closed the door behind him and whispered a silent prayer to heaven for both Tolu and Tokoni.

Tolu, when he left the Beatons' house, went straight to Nkechi, whom he knew as Tokoni's confidante. He was fortunate that Nkechi was home. He gave her Tokoni's letter to read, but Nkechi wouldn't give him any clue.

"Honestly, Nkechi, I am going to travel next week. There are so many things to do that I won't have time to go looking for her. I only want to have her address so that I can write to her," Tolu pleaded.

"I'm sorry, Tolu, but I can't tell you where she is. I gave her my word. Her mother told you that if you feel like writing to her, she will pass on your letters," Nkechi said.

"But that will take too much time. Imagine me, writing from my station. From there it will be taken to Sokoto, then to Lagos before her mother will get it and post it to her wherever she is. That will take all of four weeks," Tolu argued.

"But it's the only alternative."

"What about her job?" Tolu asked. "Has she resigned?"

"I don't know," Nkechi lied. She couldn't look at him.

"You know. You just don't want to tell me. I know, she's gone to Port Harcourt. It's the only place she knows apart from Lagos. I know she has. Oh, if only I knew her grandparents' name and address."

"You are only guessing, Tolu. She could go abroad if she wanted to, you know. So you can't be sure she is in Port Harcourt or anywhere in Nigeria," Nkechi stalled.

That jolted Tolu. He had not thought of Tokoni going abroad. But now that Nkechi had mentioned it, he knew it was possible. Oh, the whole thing was a mess.

"Nkechi," he said, "why didn't you talk to her? How could this decision of hers help the situation? If anything, it will only cause us both more sorrow."

"I know. I told her, but she would not listen. She had it all worked out. You know her too," Nkechi told him.

"And how long is she going to be away for?" Tolu asked.

"I don't know. Indefinitely. Probably as long as it takes you to love a Yoruba girl and marry her," Nkechi informed him.

"Oh, God! Is that what she thinks? Does she think it's that easy? I'm sure she meant it the other way!"

"What other way?" Nkechi frowned.

"She probably means till she falls in love with an Ijaw boy. She knows I love her so much and I won't change."

"And she loves you," Nkechi reminded him, "and she won't change."

"Then why put us both through this? What came over her?" Tolu demanded.

There was no answer.

Tolu was even more confused when he left Nkechi's house. She had succeeded in making him feel Tokoni was probably out of the country. He wasn't even sure whether she was still in love with him, even though Nkechi had said she was. But he made up his mind to try her office on Monday morning and talk to that boss of hers, whom she used to get on so well with. As far as he knew, they had no branch in Port Harcourt. They possibly had one now. Tolu went home that night feeling depressed. He couldn't stand the party. He avoided his parents and went straight to bed.

The next day, Saturday, seemed to stretch on and on. He thought and thought of what he could do and decided he would talk to Pere and Elaye over the weekend and see whether they could help him. He didn't want to go to their house, however. He wasn't sure if he would get them at the campus since they were always going home. He decided to try anyway.

Unfortunately for him, Elaye was out. He got Pere and talked to him. All he got from him was that he had no right to break his word, though he didn't approve of what his sister had done. They argued about it for the best part of an hour before Tolu decided to give up and go back home.

The next day he called on Elaye, and this time she was in, but he should have saved himself the trouble. All the help he got from her was a promise to let Tokoni know he was going to Sokoto State that same week. And she, like Nkechi, led him to believe that Tokoni could have gone overseas. She said there was no use Tolu going to Tokoni's office to ask them questions about her whereabouts. Tokoni would be very much embarrassed and annoyed if she knew. Tolu was adamant. He promised Elaye, however, to speak to nobody but Tokoni's boss, so as not to cause a scandal.

"You know what people are. If you go and start

asking more than two of them, they'll make a big story out of it. Before you know it, the rumor will spread like wildfire all over the place that she's jilted you or something like that. Please, if you must ask, choose somebody respectable who can keep his mouth closed."

Tolu agreed. When he got to Skyways Interior Decorators on Monday morning, he asked for Mr. Bamuza, Tokoni's boss. The receptionist, an attractive young woman with lips painted red, flashed her big eyes at him. She looked him up and down, not correctly but with intense appraisal, before asking him what business he had with Mr. Bamuza. Tolu told her it was personal. She gave him another critical look and shrugged her shoulders before calling Mr. Bamuza on the intercom. She had probably decided that Tolu was not worth bothering about since he didn't give her more than the most impersonal glance. He was handsome, but she had no time for all these young boys who didn't know how to treat a lady. Mr. Bamuza asked her to send the visitor up, even though he knew nobody by the name of Dr. Tolulope Johnson. She dropped the telephone and directed Tolu to the boss's office.

Mr. Bamuza's office was most impressive. The walls were painted in cool ice cream tones, and the floor was thickly carpeted. On either side of his desk were real elephant tusks. On the walls, there were major modern paintings, and an unusual jungle scene was painted on the wall directly behind Mr. Bamuza's desk. He indicated with a wave of his hand that Tolu should take one of the black leather armchairs and said, "What can I do for you, young man?"

"I am sorry to bother you, sir. My name is Tolulope Johnson. I am a medical practitioner at the L.U.T.H. I am Tokoni Beaton's fiancé."

"Oh, that's right. I'm pleased to meet you." Mr. Bamuza greeted Tolu warmly and shook hands with him a second time.

"I have come to ask you for a favor, sir, and I hope you will help me. Tokoni, as you know, has gone away, and she has left no forwarding address for me. I wonder—hem—I wonder if you can give me her address?" Tolu explained.

"I am sorry, but I couldn't do that. Our policy here is to protect the interests of our employees. If Miss Beaton had wanted you to have her address, she would have given it to you..."

"You don't understand, sir. There was some disagreement, but it's nothing we can't talk over. She has taken a rash decision by going away, and it will only make the matter worse. I promise you, if you let me know where she is, I won't go there to molest her or anything like that. I am going away on Saturday myself, and I don't have enough time to go and start looking for her. I only want to write to her," Tolu pleaded.

"I'm sorry, Dr. Johnson. Why don't you go and ask Miss Beaton's mother? She could help you, I'm sure," Mr. Bamuza offered.

"No, I have been there, and she can't help. But could you tell me one thing, Mr. Bamuza? Is she still working for you?"

"Yes. She is," Mr. Bamuza replied.

"Ah, that means she is in Nigeria. Could you tell me what branch, please?" Tolu asked again.

"Dr. Johnson, I wish I could help you, but before Miss Beaton left, she left instructions that her whereabouts should be made known to no one. You could ask people who work in this department, and they won't be able to tell you where she is. Her transfer was processed with the minimum official formalities," Mr. Bamuza explained.

"But you could help me if you wanted, sir. Please do—just tell me her address. I assure you, I won't bother her. I'm going to Sokoto State for my Youth Service Corps at the end of the week myself, so there'll be no time. I just want to write to her."

Mr. Solomon Bamuza sighed and tapped his mustache. He wished he could help Tolu, but he could not betray Tokoni's confidence, however much he sympathized with him. She had told him everything, so he knew how things were between her and this young man. He himself believed that a marriage without the consent of the parents of both parties was bound to fail. Even though he would miss Tokoni's efficient services, he was glad she had gone away. It was best. They might both meet other people and realize that this thing called love is what you make of it.

Aloud he said, "My dear young man, I'm sorry, but there's nothing in the world you'll say to me that will make me give you Tokoni Beaton's address or even tell you where she is in this country. But listen to me. I'm an elderly man, and my first son is almost as old as you. If your parents don't approve of this girl, and because of that she has gone away, leave her. Let her be. The parting won't be too painful, I assure you, since you are going away yourself too."

"Sir, I don't know for how long she's going to be away. Don't you know that's the most difficult part of it?" Tolu broke in.

"I know, but why don't you try to forget her for some time at least and give other girls a chance? Maybe you'll realize you are missing something. On the other hand, maybe she herself will miss you so much, she'll come back to you. But for now, just leave her alone," Mr. Bamuza advised.

Tolu didn't feel better after his talk with Mr. Bamuza, but he decided to take the older man's advice. After all, he had tried his best. She had no right to take such a drastic decision just because of all those silly tiffs they'd been having. He wouldn't even say they were rows. They were only trifles, and she knew why he was always in such bad moods. Nobody who lived in the sort of atmosphere in his house would be in a good mood, however cheerful they naturally might be. He lived with his parents like two women sharing the same husband. The cold war between them was getting more intense with each passing day. His parents were the cause of all this, and he felt still more resentment towards them.

But how could Tokoni be so cruel? he asked himself for the umpteenth time since Friday evening. He knew that without her address, he would be going on a wild-goose chase if he decided to go and search for her in a big city like Port Harcourt. For all he knew, there could be about a dozen Tokoni Beatons in Rivers State, though there would be just one working for Skyways Interior Decorators.

They had not been very helpful at their headquarters here in Lagos. Mr. Bamuza would not tell him if they had a branch in Port Harcourt, so on his way out, he had asked Red Lips, the receptionist. She asked him dryly why he had not asked Mr. Bamuza. He had felt like slapping her and stalked out.

Why should Tokoni put him to all this trouble and worry?

If she had been hard done by, wasn't he experiencing the same? Did she think he was happy with the way things were? This was what his friends were always saying about loving a girl too much. He could remember Deji Ariyo saying, some weeks ago, "Who loves more, the man or the woman? I'd rather love a woman less than she loves me. Once you love her as much as she loves you, that's her passport to ruling your life. The next thing you know, she'll have you taking her orders and obeying her commands."

Tolu had argued that not all girls were like that. "Take Tokoni for instance," he had argued. "She loved him just as much as he loved her, and she never tried to rule him. She took his feelings into consideration and respected him, taking great care not to oppose him in public." The rest of his friends had laughed and said he should wait and see. It was only a matter of time before she changed. Women were like that, all goody-goody, sweetness and light when they were courted. As soon as they got the much-coveted ring on their finger, and become your Mrs., they become real madams in the true sense of the word.

"Old boy, don't trust a woman that much," Soji had advised.

"But you have to.

Trust is the start of it,

Joy is a part of it,

and Love is the heart of it," he had argued.

"Bobo Ke!" They had all cheered and laughed at him. They would all probably say, "We told you so!" now. As Mr. Bamuza said, he would leave Tokoni for the time being. She probably was not sure what her feelings for him were anymore. But she had signed her letter "all the love in my heart." That must mean she still cared. It was her usual way of signing her letters to him. She still must care. What they had together, the love between them, was not one that could wither so easily. Maybe she would miss him too, as much as he would miss her.

By the time he finished his service, they would have sorted things out and come back together. Yes, he would leave her alone. It wouldn't be too bad, as Mr. Bamuza said, since he wouldn't be in Lagos himself. Life would have been unbearable for him if he were to be in Lagos, he knew that. That girl meant more than anybody in the whole world to him. He could not begin to imagine how he would get on without her. But she had taken this decision, and he would let her be.

He could not really rule out the possibility of there being somebody else in her life, like that Ebitimi for instance. The guy was just too smooth and too friendly with Tokoni for his liking. And he knew that he was in love with Tokoni and had so much to offer her. Not that Tolu had nothing himself, but if he went against his parents' wish and married Tokoni, he was sure they would not leave him a kobo. He wouldn't worry while she was with him. All he cared about, apart from her, was his job. He realized it was the only security he had and made sure he did his best. Tokoni was just being silly, giving his parents the upper hand. How could he start now to forget her and look for an eligible girl as his parents would say?

As for that Doyin Akano, the student nurse he took out occasionally, she had no illusions about sharing his life. She knew from the start that he had a fiancée, and she didn't mind as long as he spared her the odd date or two. She knew as well as he did that as soon as he went to Sokoto, that would be the end of the line for both of them.

"She is nothing to me, and I could never compare her to Tokoni," he had told Akinola. Doyin was a beautiful girl with strongly marked features. She was sophisticated and so confident in her slightly lush good looks. She was not the type of girl you thought of keeping at home as your wife. She would grace any home beautifully but would need servants to manage it. She wasn't the type he would like to be the mother of his children. Tokoni now, she was much more in that mold, so beautiful but unassuming. Her beauty was ravishing, woven of many things, which made her sensuous in a way she did not intend. And she had spiritual loveliness. She would make a heaven for any man to come home to at the end of a hard day at work. Even at her age, she was a homemaker. She created a sense of calm and order about her. Why was he thinking about all these? He must get the girl out of his mind.

Tolu was so busy in the next few days, getting his things together and shuttling between the Lagos University Teaching Hospital, where he trained and did his housemanship, and the Youth Corps Secretariat, that he had no time to think about Tokoni. It was only when he was in bed that he thought about her and how she was faring. It wasn't easy at all for him not to have an open quarrel with his parents, just at the thought of what they had done to his love life, but he restrained himself and avoided them as much as possible.

The day before he was to leave, his mother asked him casually if Tokoni would be visiting him there sometime.

"No!" Tolu snapped at her. "Why should she?"

"Forgive me, of course! I thought you two were going ahead with your plans and getting married."

Tolu thought for some seconds whether he should tell her the new turn of events but decided against it. "Yes, we are. But she is not coming over there to see me."

"I suppose you'll be coming over here often then?" his mother asked, sensing something different in her son's resigned way of talking about Tokoni.

"I don't know yet. It depends."

"On what?"

Tolu knew there was no leave as such except the one week for Convocation and two weeks after the service, but he decided to play his mother along. "What the place is like," he replied noncommittally.

The next day, he went off to Sokoto by air, and from there he went to his station by road. It was a small mission hospital, the only one for miles around. Tolu was taken to his quarters by an elderly Scotsman, who was the Senior Surgeon there. Dr. McEwen told Tolu all he needed to know and promised to introduce him to the other members of staff the next day. "I promise you'll be so busy here, you won't have time to think!" was his parting remark to Tolu, as if he knew that was just what Tolu wanted.

CHAPTER SIX

Tokoni rarely went out in Port Harcourt. She was very lonely when she first got there, but gradually she came to know a few of her colleagues in the office, along with other members of her extended family. It wasn't too bad. Every day, she sat at home, reading or talking to her grandparents. The only time she went out, apart from going to work, was after church on Sundays when she went with her grandmother to visit one relation or the other. Occasionally, her grandfather accompanied them too. She was always being urged by Ina, as her grandmother was fondly called, to go out more. She tried to do so but found herself thinking every time of Tolu. She missed him a lot, and she kept wondering if he was missing her too. She spoke to her family on the phone every other Sunday evening, but they never told her anything about him, except once, when Elaye had informed her that he was going somewhere in Sokoto State. She knew from Nkechi's letters that he had already gone there. She also wondered how his family took her going away. She guessed they would be relieved more than anything else. She longed to ask for news about him but refused to ask any member of her family or Nkechi. She was out here to give him a chance to forget her, wasn't she? But as yet, she couldn't even bear to talk to another man, let alone go out with them, even though she was not short of offers.

Tolu had spoiled all men for her. She could never stop comparing them with him. Her heart was not ready for a love affair with anybody else, and no young man would want to have a platonic friendship with a girl, she was sure. It was a rare task, looking for someone as self-disciplined as Tolu, who had waited so long before making love to her. Who would court her like Tolu, anyway, like a knight of old on a white horse? She missed him. She missed him so much. She would give anything to have his arms around her, to hear him tell her in his deep, gentle voice that all would be well. She had not known it would be this rough, and she was half regretting the step she had taken. It was eight weeks since she left Lagos, and she had not heard from him. Had she covered her tracks so well, or was he respecting her wishes more closely than she had really intended? Had Tolu forgotten her already?

"Has he found somebody else out there in Sokoto," she wondered, "or is he still getting himself settled?" She would be glad for his sake if he had found someone else. If the girl was someone his parents approved of, then they could both live happily ever after.

She shook herself out of her reverie and said wordlessly, trying to convince herself, "I'm glad I came out here. He has already forgotten me, I'm sure. I don't regret anything." The words gave her no comfort.

A few days later, she got some letters from home. She recognized Tolu's handwriting on one of the envelopes and quickly tore it open. Her heartbeat became so loud that she was sure, if there had been anybody else in the room, they would have heard it. She had been so worried about Tolu that she could not help being glad to hear from him at last.

Tokoni, my love,

I've kept silent all this time because it's what you wished. I've tried to forget you as you requested, but can one forget one's life? You are my life, my whole being, my joy and my strength. Your serenity was the force behind my successes. Without you, my life is a mess. I can never make anything out of it.

Tokoni, why did you take such a dreadful decision? I keep on asking myself, but there is no answer. For almost two months now, I have neither seen nor heard from you, and it's been like two years to me. It would have been bad enough if I knew you were coming back, but to think you have walked right out of my life is unbearable. It was the strain, as you know quite well, that made me behave in such a way to you. I was not myself. Now I've learned my lesson, and I promise you that it will never happen again.

I know there is no cruelty in you. I know you left because you thought it was the best thing to do in the circumstances. But Tokoni, you should at least have allowed me to voice my opinion on the matter. You are marrying me, not my parents. I promise you that, if you love me (which I know you do) just a tiny bit, things will be all right. We won't stay under the same roof with them. There is a limit to how they can behave to you in our own house. I don't care if they cut me out of their will or not. All I care about is for you, my Toks, to love me, and all I'm asking you for right now, is for you to come back.

I am currently doing my National Youth Service in Sokoto State. It is a small mission hospital and has a staff of less than twenty people. There are only five doctors, and so we have a pretty tight schedule here. What about you? I believe you are still with Skyways Interior Decorators, but I am not too sure since nobody is ready to volunteer any information. I hope you are doing fine anyway.

Tokoni, I know you are missing me just as much as I'm missing you. I don't understand why you choose to make us both suffer like this. Please reply to this letter and let me know when you'll be coming back to Lagos. I love you.

Your loving,

Tolu.

Tokoni was crying as she read this letter. She read it again and again, and she cried and cried. So he had not forgotten her after all. She had thought she was doing Tolu good by leaving him, but it seemed she was only causing both of them unnecessary agony. He did not say what his parents thought of this separation. If they knew, they would be glad and relieved. Tolu did not mention their opinion, she decided, because he did not want to hurt her more than necessary. She would not go back on her decision anyway, not while they were so adverse to marriage between her and Tolu.

What sort of family would theirs be if she had children and they were not allowed to go and see their paternal grandparents? It would break Tolu himself if his parents disowned him or refused to acknowledge his wife. Even though Tolu thought he could not care less now, she herself would not want it. It would be too much burden for her conscience to bear. She thought of writing and telling him so, but then she reminded herself of her decision not to communicate with him. She put the letter away in her vanity case and tried to put it out of her mind. This decision unnerved and unsettled her, even though it was hers. She felt angry with society for being so petty and treating her like this. She needed an outlet for her feelings, so she vented her anger on her mother, who spoke to her on the phone the following day.

"Why did you pass on the letter, Mummy, Tolu's letter, after what I told you?"

"I couldn't refuse him, dear, and anyway, he

sent it by post. The last time I saw him... that was on the day you left... he was desperately worried," her mother explained and added, "Will you reply?"

"No, I won't. And tell him not to write to me again," Tokoni replied.

"I don't know where he is, but I suppose he told you in his letter, so you can give him that message yourself. Ah-ha, that's too much to ask of anybody. It's like beating a child and asking him not to cry," her mother scolded her.

"Oh, don't bother. I know what to do," Tokoni snapped.

Her mother knew better than to ask.

Tokoni did not reply to the letter, and after another month, Mrs. Beaton got a phone call from Tolu in Sokoto. He asked whether Tokoni had got the letter or not. Mrs. Beaton told him she had but would rather not reply.

Tolu was disappointed. What had he done to deserve this? he wondered. He knew he had been pretty much under strain and easily irritated just before Tokoni left, but there had never been a showdown, a big quarrel between them, because she had always tried to be cool, however much he had tried to bait her. He decided once again that he would leave Tokoni alone. He would not write to her anymore, and he would try to forget about her as she suggested. But could he? This girl had been so much a part of him. How could he not help but think of her? And at the hospital, there was not much social life. He had nothing to do after work but think and read, and the former took up the better part of his time. There were lots of pretty girls among the nurses, but he only greeted them and joked flippantly with them like all the others did. He had eyes for only one girl, and that girl was out of his reach. As for Doyin, he hadn't written to her since he got there, and even though she sent him lovely postcards, he made it a point of duty not to reply. He knew she would soon get herself a new boyfriend if she hadn't done so yet. Why couldn't he forget this Tokoni girl, he kept on asking himself? After all, she was the one who took the decision to leave him, and hadn't he tried his best to get in touch with her?

"Take a grip on yourself, old boy. Forget about her for the time being, at least while you are out here, away from city life."

One evening, Tolu was in the hospital grounds taking a stroll when he came across Jummai Luka, a pretty Fulani Staff Nurse, dressed in full traditional Fulani regalia, with a gold headband glittering on her forehead. She stopped in front of him and said, "Hello," with a shy little smile.

"Hello. Where are you off to?" Tolu asked her.

"Oh, there's a Kadan Kadan dance at the village center, and I thought I should go," she informed him, the jade pendants of her earrings swinging against her fair cheeks.

"What's a Kadan Kadan dance?" Tolu asked

and stared at her while she explained. Kadan Kadan meant "Small Small," and it was the name of a popular Sokoto dance, in which men and women stood on separate lines and danced facing each other, shaking their waists and bending their knees. He had never really noticed before that Staff Nurse Luka had such a beautiful body. He knew she had a lovely face and a skin as fine as porcelain, but he had never realized that she had such a perfect body. Nothing he had ever seen her wear had suited her so well or made her look so flower-like.

"Would you like to come along with me, Dr. Johnson?" he heard her ask.

"Oh yes, if you don't mind and if it's going to be fun," Tolu replied, glad to get away from himself and his thoughts for a few hours.

On the way to the village, he found Jummai such an interesting person to talk to. He felt he'd known her almost all his life as she told him about their various dances and customs. He did not enjoy the Kadan Kadan dance much, but he enjoyed Jummai's company a lot. He watched as she tapped her small feet to the music and nodded her head to the rhythm, her oriental jewelry adding more music to the dance. Her pointed nose was pierced, and the little hole held a small ring, which made her look like an Indian goddess in the moonlight. Tolu wondered why he had never taken more notice of this tall, willowy girl the four months he'd been there. From now on, he decided, he was going to befriend this girl with the infectious laughter and make his time here worthwhile. She was such good company. From then on, he spent all his spare time with her, going to visit places of interest in and around the village.

Jummai spent a lot of her time in Tolu's little flat but made sure she usually left before dark, as the mere rumor that she was in his flat till late in the night would have distressed her parents so much. The whole hospital soon knew about their friendship, and somehow it survived the usual "nine days wonder" of hospital gossip and developed into something warmer. Jummai was very tactful. She told those people who cared enough to ask her that the relationship between her and Tolu was clearly platonic. Very soon, the fact that they were mere friends was widely spread through the same grapevine that started the rumor. She liked Tolu a lot, and she knew he was in love with some girl, even though he told her nothing about it.

Once, when she was helping him to clean up his room, she had found Tokoni's last letter to him and had read it out of sheer curiosity. She didn't know the story behind it, but she knew that if she had been in this Tokoni's shoes, she would have fought Tolu's parents to the last. She would not have left him unless he had asked her to go. She knew Tolu still loved Tokoni very much. She knew what Tokoni looked like. On Tolu's bedside table, there was a large framed color photo of a beautiful, smiling girl. She knew without anybody telling her, this was Tokoni, and there were more photographs of this same girl inside the drawer.

Jummai felt so sorry for both Tolu and Tokoni.

Reading between the lines of Tokoni's letter, she knew the problem was tribal discrimination. It made her glad that they were nothing more than friends who enjoyed each other's company. She wished, however, that she could help him forget Tokoni. During the day, she tried her best to get him interested in a lot of things to stop him brooding, but even that did not help much. Sometimes she would be talking to him without any reply, and then she would look at him, only to realize he wasn't even with her. He was far away and had not heard a word of what she was saying. She wondered what sort of girl this was that could wield so much influence over a man like Tolu, leaving him so morose sometimes in spite of his natural cheerfulness. She also wondered how long they had been together before this breakup. How she wished Tolu would confide in her, but he would not. He never even accidentally mentioned her name to Jummai's hearing, and once when she had asked him about his girlfriend in Lagos, he had snapped at her.

This afternoon, she waited for him in his little flat, knowing that he had probably forgotten she had promised to bring him a special lunch. He had told her he loved Yam Pottage but hadn't tasted it since he came, so feeling sorry for him, she had promised to cook him some for lunch. But she had to leave at 1:20 p.m. as she was on afternoon duty. She left a brief note for him and went home to change for work, hoping he would come home early enough to eat the food while it still tasted nice.

Tolu turned the key in the door of his little flat, yawning, and rushed into his sitting room, only to find it empty. He went along straight to the kitchen and found a note beside a covered dish on his dining table. He had been talking to Dr. Laila and Dr. McEwen and had forgotten until ten minutes ago that Jummai was supposed to bring him lunch. He opened the dish, and the delicious aroma of the Yam Pottage made him realize he was hungry. He had only had a cup of tea for breakfast and nothing since. How nice Jummai was, he reflected, grateful for her friendship. He felt the bottom of the plate and found the food still warm, so he decided against heating it up. As he ate, he remembered the note and tore it open. Jummai was a stickler for convention. Even little notes like this were put in envelopes.

She was such an undemanding, generous, friendly, and likable girl. She asked no questions and was happy to take each day as it came. That was exactly the type of girl he needed at this stage in his affairs. He finished eating his meal and went into his sitting room to relax with a bottle of beer. As he sat down, he found a couple of letters on his desk. He did not have much personal mail since he came out here, but then he was not exactly a dutiful correspondent of late. Apart from his emotional problems, there was so much to do at the hospital. It was the only one for miles around, and most people came a long, long way, only to complain about common ailments. They were mostly illiterates and had stopped doing any form of self-diagnosis ever since the hospital was opened. Those who were really ill refused to come to the hospital but stayed at home, fading away until relatives rushed them down at the last minute when little could be done for them. He had been called to the beds of sick people four times that week, four uninterrupted nights in a row, and he had only worked hard, trying to resuscitate two of them who had gone already.

Life there was hectic. It was the sort of work he needed, the sort of work that brought true forgetfulness, but still, he needed more, especially on the nights when there were no interruptions and nothing else to do. There never seemed to be time for him to do things like letter writing anyway. He looked at the letters. There was one from his mother, who wrote once a month, and another from his favorite cousin, who must have got his address from his mother. He hadn't written to anybody in his family except his parents since he came out. He opened his cousin's first, eager to know what Kayus had to say. It was a short letter, asking how he was and telling him he would be getting married. Would Tolu be able to make the wedding, since it was the Saturday before his Convocation ceremony? Tolu then opened his mother's letter. She told him as usual that both of them were well and that they missed him. They hadn't seen him for six whole months, she had written, and were looking forward to having him home for the Convocation ceremony. Was it six months since he came, Tolu wondered. It seemed as if he'd been there for over one year. He surely must spend in Lagos the whole week due to him for his Convocation.

Anyway, his mother concluded, "I hope you'll be able to make it for Kayus' wedding. I understand you will have started your one week's leave for Convocation by then. It's going to be a grand affair. The whole family will be coming, even brother Toyin from London."

Tolu decided he would not go for any wedding. He did not think he could stand all those good-humored questions about when it would be his turn and how could he come to the wedding without a girl. Those would even be better than the well-meant prayers from the older people, who would be full of sympathy because he was sure they must have heard about what was happening. He was surprised that his mother, in all her letters, had made no mention of Tokoni. Knowing her, he felt sure if she had heard anything about Tokoni leaving, she would have said so or made some comment about it. So far, she hadn't. Neither had his father, who had written twice or so. He was not looking forward to going to Lagos. He would find it really lonely without Tokoni, but life must go on. Whether he liked it or not, one day he would have to go back to Lagos. But how he wished he could forget Tokoni. Would the thought of her always have the power to hurt him so?

He decided to post a letter to her when he got to Lagos. This time he decided he would take it through her office.

Tolu decided to go home two days after his cousin's wedding. His parents were very happy to see him and, of course, his mother wanted to fatten him up. She scarcely left the kitchen during the whole of Tolu's stay. She made him look at himself in the mirror, exclaiming emotionally at the tired lines on his face. "What have you been doing to yourself? Don't you eat at all?" she asked worriedly. "You have to take care of yourself and stop over-working."

His father was more reserved in his observations and comments. He looked hard at Tolu for a long time and knew that things were not well, but he said nothing.

The day after Tolu got home, he went to see his cousin Kayus and his new wife. He had a nice enough time with them and went to check on Doyin Akano, his one-time student-nurse girl, who he gathered from Kayus' wife, was now a Staff Nurse. He was told she was on night duty and would not resume until 9 p.m. Then he called on Tokoni's mother, but she was not in, so he went home.

Tolu was surprised to see Folake Cadmus, the daughter of one of his mother's best friends, in his house when he came in. He hadn't seen her for a long time, as she had been studying in America, and he didn't know she had come back home. "Hello, Folake! When did you come back?" he greeted her warmly.

"Hi, Tolu. I came back two months ago," she replied with a faint American accent.

"Oh, it's good to see you. Have you finished now?" Tolu asked her.

"Yes, I'm serving here in Lagos at NICON. I hear you are serving somewhere in the North."

"Yes, in Sokoto State. I..."

"Oh, Tolu, you are back." His mother came in, obviously from the kitchen, wiping her hands with a napkin.

"Yes, Mama," Tolu replied, staring at Folake's long, lovely legs crossed under her as she sat comfortably on the settee.

"You remember Folake, don't you?" his mother went on. "I don't think you've seen her since she was a teenager, but now she's grown up to be such a beauty, hasn't she? A beauty with brains too!" Mrs. Johnson smiled at Folake indulgently then, avoiding Tolu's eyes, declared she had to go and finish the meal. She was preparing something special.

Folake offered to help, but she insisted she needed no help. "You stay and talk to Tolu. I'll join you when I finish. You two must have a lot in common," and she dashed off to the kitchen.

Tolu felt embarrassed at his mother's too-obvious tactics. He hoped this beautiful young girl did not think he couldn't find his own girlfriends.

But as if reading his thoughts, Folake said with a grimace, "Mothers! Boy, are they a menace! They try eternally, don't you think? My mother would have me married off before I know what is happening to me."

Tolu smiled and said, "I'm glad you understand.

117

A beautiful girl like you won't be short of boyfriends."

"Oh sure, but you know I'm so much out of circulation about here, I need to be re-introduced."

"You mean you haven't been hooked? What were all those boys over there doing?"

"Well, actually, there was this guy, but he got married to a black American just before I came back." Folake shrugged. "That's love and life."

"You are pretty, Folake, much prettier than I remember you. You've got such lovely legs."

"Oh no, Tolu! Come off it. Not those long legs you used to describe as Rolf the Ganger's?" Folake laughed.

"Rolf the Ganger?" Tolu repeated, not remembering.

"You mean you could forget that? I'll remind you. Rolf the Ganger was that man you learned about in history. He had such gangly, long legs. You know he was in the same league as Attila the Hun, Eric the Red, and so on."

"Oh, that's right—those days," Tolu recalled. "You have a good memory, Folake."

She was a pretty girl even then, but her legs had seemed to be so much out of proportion to the rest of her body. Now they looked like a model's, and she was a lot prettier.

They had their meal, with his mother fussing

over Folake like a mother hen, then he had to take her home. Folake's mother received him just as well as his mother received her daughter. He knew his mother must have told Folake's mother he was unattached, and they were both expecting the two of them to fall in love with each other or something like that.

When he got back home, his father had come back from work, and they all sat down talking.

"Demola, Folake Cadmus came here today. She's such a pretty girl," his mother informed her husband. "Tolu, what do you think of her?"

"Very beautiful, but it wasn't love at second sight, Mama," Tolu replied offhandedly, and his father burst into laughter.

"Anike, let the boy be. He's only just got home," he reproached his wife.

"Hmn, okay. I wonder why you have no time for any other company except that Beaton girl. She didn't even think it necessary to call and ask how we were, all the time you were away. A Yoruba girl, if she really wanted to be our daughter-in-law, would have done so," his mother complained.

"It's not easy when she knows we don't regard her as one."

"But did she try? She didn't even bother. She doesn't care at all," she maintained.

"Anike, I told you to lay off this matter."

"But I have to say it. How can we lay off and let Tolu marry her and...?"

"You are discussing me as if I am not here. Mama, Tokoni Beaton has not been to see you because she is not in Lagos herself. I don't know where she is. Because of you, she's broken off with me. That's the way she puts it," Tolu informed them and went up to his room.

His parents were very surprised to hear that. They had discussed Tolu's love for Tokoni several times and had decided that they were both sure they did not want their son to marry a kobokobo, and anyway, not Tokoni Beaton, who was only a secretary. They wanted Tolu to marry some girl from a high-class family and one who had a university degree too. But Mr. Johnson had advised his wife to leave Tolu alone and not to say anything about Tokoni during the young man's week-long stay at home. The boy had gone away to Sokoto with bad feelings between them, and he wanted them all to be friends again before re-introducing such a matter. But now Tolu's mother had put her foot in it. Tolu's father thought in his mind that the Tokoni girl must have some hidden depths within her, to be able to take such a step. Maybe now Tolu would meet someone else and forget her.

Tolu took Folake out a number of times and enjoyed her company, but found himself comparing her with Tokoni almost all the time. He wished he could forget Tokoni and love this girl who was just as beautiful. It was not as easy as switching from one channel to another. Love was deeper than that.

Even though he knew with this girl he would have no problems, he couldn't do it. All his family would approve of Folake. He needed no one to tell him that. She was young, from a nice family, educated, respectful, and beautiful. They would all love her, but it was only Tokoni he wanted as a wife. If he could not have her, then they would have to wait until his heart was quite ready for another love.

Tolu visited Mrs. Beaton again and found her at home this time. They talked about his job and he asked of Tokoni. Mrs. Beaton told him Tokoni was well and that she had spoken to her on the phone just the Sunday before. He also went to see both Elaye and Pere. Nobody, however, would tell him what she was doing or how long she would be away. From a few hints dropped here and there, he was quite certain she was in Port Harcourt.

Two nights before he was due to go back to the North, he wrote to her. The next morning he took it to Skyways Interior Decorators and asked them to forward it to Miss Beaton in Port Harcourt.

Folake came to his Convocation, and he promised to write to her when he got back. She had helped to make his week pleasant, and he had called on most of his friends. He had had a nice time generally, but Lagos was too full of memories of one girl for him. And the lazy man-about-town life wasn't for him anymore. He needed to bury himself in work, and the hospital was the answer. As for his parents, they made no more mention of Tokoni after that first day, and he was glad.

CHAPTER SEVEN

Tolu's second letter got to Tokoni in the office, but eager as she was, she hardened her heart and decided not to read it until she got home. She had gone about her duty calmly all the while she had been in Port Harcourt, but deep down, her heart was in pieces. She had become a woman, and a sad one at that, one who knew the meaning of love and sorrow and disillusionment. She had grown thinner because she was worried and unhappy, even though her relations were marvelous. They tried their best to make her happy and to forget her sorrow. She never went out with people of her own age and refused any invitations and turned down any advances made towards her. She had become wary. She wouldn't allow herself to think of any other man. She heard so little about Tolu that this letter made her heart lighter even before she had read it. She went through her work like a robot and rushed home.

As she sat in one corner of the staff van on her way home, she compared the traffic here to that of Lagos. Lagos seemed like another world away. At 4 p.m. on a Wednesday like this, any main road would be jammed with traffic, the cars crawling like tortoises, and the people streaming out of nowhere like bees, sweating and scrambling for buses and taxis for all they were worth. But out here, it was different. There was no traffic jam except on Fridays when people went to their villages, and there was no scramble for transport. The buses were regular and nearly always empty, since most people traveled by taxis as they were quite cheap. In Lagos, you dared not think of chartering a taxi unless you were rolling in money. Even a "drop" was not cheap. Oh, she had to admit, life here would have been pleasant if only she were happy.

Tolu's letter said:

"If you could see me now, Tokoni, you wouldn't feel that absence from me is the best way we can solve this problem. I'm no longer the person you left behind in Lagos. I can't stop thinking about you. I'm going out of my mind. Tokoni, please come back. I haven't seen or heard from you for almost seven months now, and I haven't forgotten you. You are always in my thoughts and dreams. I shall never forget you, because I love you as much as life itself. I know you must be very unhappy too, unless you have already forgotten me. Why are you letting my parents win? They are already one up on us. They are winning the battle unless you come back. Please, Toks, think about it and come back. I can't lie to you and say they have given their consent, but with you beside me, we shall work something out together.

Tokoni, please reply even if you are not coming back. Yours desperately,

Tolu."

Tokoni held Tolu's letter to her breast and cried. It was saddening for her to know that he still cared so much for her. She wondered what he had been doing to make him say that if she saw him now, she wouldn't know he was the same Tolu. She had and still wanted only the best for him, but now it looked as if she was ruining his happiness. She wasn't happy herself. Most nights she cried herself to sleep, wondering if she had done the right thing by him. How she wished falling in and out of love was as easy as switching programs. Tolu's letters always left her with such guilt in her heart. She was longing for him, and he was unhappy without her. But while his parents remained adamantly opposed to the marriage, she had to consider that all was lost. She wondered if there was any girl in his life yet. She wouldn't deceive herself that he was the stuff celibates were made of.

A few days later, she was alone in her room reading when she heard a knock on her door.

"Come in, Ina," she said quietly.

Ina, her grandmother, came in and smiled at the young girl lying on the bed and remembered her own daughter at this age. Tokoni and her mother were as like as two peas in a pod.

"Hello, Tokoni. You knew it was me?"

"Yes, I knew. You always do everything so softly," Tokoni smiled back.

"Hum, Tokoni, always reading! You could open a bookshop with all the books you've bought since you got here, you know."

Tokoni smiled and said nothing.

"Anyway, I've come to talk to you about something," her grandmother continued.

"I hope it's not serious."

"It's not very serious, but it's serious all the same," the old lady said, and went straight to the point. "Tokoni, I never meant to interfere or probe into your life, but I've noticed you are not at all happy. Many mornings, I look into your eyes and I know you've cried yourself to sleep the night before. Your mother told me you came out here to forget somebody, but it's obvious you have not succeeded. You are only young once, and I hate to see you like this. You still have a long way to go in your life. Your refusing all other advances is not going to help you at all. You've got to learn to take things in your stride. Don't let this one bad experience disillusion you or end your belief in love. Do you love this boy so much? Is that it? There's nothing one can't get over. You'll get over it. This is just a matter of time..."

She stopped as she saw tears trickling down the young girl's cheeks. "What!" she exclaimed. "You've started crying already? Do you care to tell me about it? Don't cry, there'll be other men. You are young, and youth is resilient."

"Everybody keeps telling me that, but I can't

seem to be able to forget him. Oh, Ina, I love him so much, but his parents hate me. Heaven knows I've tried to forget him, but it's no use, and he has not forgotten me either."

Tokoni then told her grandmother, between sobs, everything that had happened.

Mrs. Biriye could see that Tokoni had really taken after her side of the family, just like her mother, Marie. They were all "one-man women," loving only once and with a burning passion. At almost seventy, Ere-Ebi Biriye still loved her husband as much as when they were newlyweds. She knew this young girl had a difficult problem on her hands, unlike her mother who in those days, because Stephen had ignored her twice, had thought she had a problem. Her heart ached for Tokoni. She soothed and comforted her as she cried, as she used to comfort Marie.

"Tokoni," she said gently, "that's enough. You must reply, if just to tell him you are well. You are hurting him so much, and yourself even more. Don't worry, all will be well. Now, do go to sleep and don't cry anymore. Pray to the Lord to help you always. Good night, my child."

Ere-Ebi Biriye went to bed, with her young granddaughter on her mind. Tokoni was still only a child, and these problems should have been beyond her, the old lady thought sadly, but such was life and love. None of her other nine grandchildren had such problems with their partners. They had all got married to Ijaws except for her grandson Ebikabi, who married an Igbo girl, her granddaughter Preye, who married a Kalabari boy, and her granddaughter Bindo, who married an Itsekiri. Bindo was the only one who had any problems, and they weren't serious. They were all happily married and she now had fifteen great-grandchildren. She prayed fervently for Tokoni that night, so that she would soon find happiness.

Tokoni decided to take Ina's advice. After that second letter, she pondered whether to send him just a little note. Ina had finally decided for her. She wasted no time before writing the letter. She pondered over the words, wondering how best she could write to him without raising his hopes high about her coming back to him. She tore the first draft because she felt it was too suggestive and intimate. She found it very difficult to write a casual letter to Tolu, after what they had been to each other. The second one was as brief as possible.

Tolu,

I got both your letters. I don't want you to write me anymore. As it is, I don't think there is any future for me in your family. I am fine. Please try to forget me. Think about your parents and consider their happiness as well as yours. Remember you are their only child. I always remember you in my prayers.

Yours,

Tokoni.

Tolulope Johnson was very happy when he got this letter. He looked at the postmark and saw that it was from Port Harcourt. Hadn't he thought as much? She could not have gone anywhere but to her grandparents in Port Harcourt. A pity he did not know their address, and that this had happened when he was in the Youth Service Corps. He had been brought up to take his duty so seriously that he could not leave work and go to search for her. He was disappointed when he read the letter. It was so curt and to the point, no more than a note actually, but he consoled himself that there was still hope. If not, Tokoni would have cut off from him completely.

He would never have believed it, had somebody told him, that she had such a strong streak of determination in her. However, he knew she still loved him. She must! They had had too many good times together for her to forget him so soon. He would not believe that she did not love him anymore. All the same, the last ounce of fight left him. There was no point in going on about her, thinking about her all the time, and letting memories of her spoil his relationship with other girls. He stopped moping and spent his time with Jummai and her friends and his only other love— medicine, its knowledge and practice. He spent all his spare time absorbing every book or journal about every medical subject that he could get his hand on.

When he was in Lagos, he had had a talk with his friend, Akinola, who had advised him to leave

Tokoni for a while, but he had not listened. Now he realized that it was the best way. He would play it her way. He was glad Jummai was such an undemanding and understanding girl and happy all her friends now knew they were merely friends, not lovers. She had told him that very soon her marriage would be arranged, and he was happy for her. She deserved to be happy.

Ebitimi Ifie came like a ray of sunshine into Tokoni's humdrum existence. He had taken a month's leave from work and had decided to spend it in Port Harcourt, to look up Tokoni and plead his cause with her again. Tokoni was very happy to see him. He was from home, and she clutched every word he had to say as news of her family and friends. Ebitimi, on the other hand, was surprised to see how changed Tokoni was. She looked so much thinner than when she was in Lagos, and her eyes were so sad. How he wished he could bring some light into those eyes and a real smile instead of that faint opening of the lips. He decided he would try even if he did not succeed. Both her grandparents, who knew his father, welcomed him nicely, and when he announced he hadn't eaten, her grandmother said she would dish up something for him quickly.

"When did your flight arrive here?" Tokoni's grandfather asked conversationally.

"Just 4:30 p.m. Then I went to my uncle's house in Trans Amadi Layout, dropped my things, and came straight here."

"I'm so pleased to see you, Ebitimi," Tokoni said. "You are looking so well."

"Which is more than I can say for you. What is happening to you, Tokoni?" Ebitimi wondered.

"Good thing you asked, my son. Don't you see how thin she is? Her mother, if she sees her, will believe we don't feed her. It's all because she thinks so much; she thinks too much, this little girl," Ina said, shaking her head sadly and looking pointedly at Tokoni.

"Don't worry, Ina. All that will change now. I don't know Port Harcourt very well, and I'm expecting her to show me around while I'm here," Ebitimi said.

"Ah, where does she know in this Port Harcourt, this one? She stays at home every day of the week, all the time she doesn't have to go to work. It's only when I force her to come out with me to visit one or the other of her uncles or cousins that this girl goes out of this house. And then we go to church on Sundays. That's all."

"Ina, this is not fair. You are discussing me as if I'm not here. I go to work, remember?" Tokoni protested.

"Do you call going to work 'going out'? Tell me, my son, do you call going to work 'going out'?" Ina asked Ebitimi.

"Of course not, Ma. We have to go to work, if we are not self-employed, whether we like it or not..." Ebitimi stated.

Dada, as her grandfather was fondly called, was enjoying this conversation, but he decided to rescue Tokoni all the same. He remembered Marie, when she was a young girl. She had always been on the receiving end of her mother's tongue, and he had been the one who rescued her every time.

"Well, my dear," he said with a chuckle, "it's not as if they are lying, you know. All they've said so far is the truth. You think too much, and you never go out with people of your own age, I mean. But then, Ina, don't go on about it. Leave her alone."

"And watch her fade away like a little flower?" Ina countered.

"Don't worry, Ina. I know the tonic she needs, but since she can't have it, I'm the next best thing. I assure you, she's going to be all right in no time at all. Take my word," Ebitimi told Ina confidently.

Ebitimi came every day after that. Sometimes they went out together to the movies or just out for a drink or to see some of his relatives. He made her laugh so much that she did not regret his coming at all. She could talk to him about how she felt. He listened patiently to her while she talked about Tolu and said nothing about his own feelings. When she looked at him, she always saw this wistful expression on his nice, handsome face, and she wished there was something she could do. She wished she could forget Tolu, fall out of love with him, and fall in love with Ebitimi, but it was impossible. She wasn't going to be able to forget him yet, if ever she would.

Ebitimi Ifie fitted in quite comfortably in Tokoni's family circle in Port Harcourt, especially with her grandmother, who thought the world of him. Ere-Ebi Biriye wished fervently that Tokoni had been in love with him. Marriage between Tokoni and Ebitimi would have been super. He was

such an easy-going and uncomplicated, good-
humored young man. But you can't trust the heart to
fall for the sort of man you want. She knew that
every woman has an ideal, an idea of the sort of
man she wants to marry. When you fall in love, you
forget about all those ideals. Oh, but wouldn't it
have been nice if Ebitimi was marrying Tokoni?

Soon the month was over, and Ebitimi had to
go back to Lagos. He had not said a word to Tokoni
about how he felt. He knew she was aware of it, and
he was not going to rush her. She had opened up
and told him everything, and he knew there was
such an emptiness. She was in a state when it would
be terribly easy to turn to someone else, just as an
escape from her thoughts. Her loneliness was so
very great that it would be really tempting if he
started declaring his love for her at this stage. He
did not want Tokoni on the rebound. He wanted her
with the sort of love and passion she had for Tolu.
He could not imagine him marrying her while she
still felt that way about another man. It would kill
his pride. He was content to wait and see how
things turn out.

His parting from her was almost tearful, but for
his good-humored nature. He had taken her to
dinner at the Olympia Hotel, and they had enjoyed
each other's company and the meal. When they
were saying goodbye, he stopped abruptly and drew
her close. So far, he hadn't been passionate in his
embraces, but tonight, he decided, was going to be
different. He drew her close, and she went willingly
into his arms, probably because it was such a long

time since she felt a man's arms about her. She was breathless when he released her.

"That was some goodbye!" she said lightly.

"Yes," he agreed. "It's to ensure that you will miss me."

"Of course I shall, with or without that," Tokoni admitted shyly.

"For good measure, I shall do it again. I won't let anybody or anything touch my mouth until I get back to Lagos. Then I shall kiss your mother and say it's from you!" Ebitimi grinned and kissed her again.

Tokoni wished yet again that she could love Ebitimi. She was so fond of him, and surely fondness could grow into love, but still she couldn't do it. Tolulope Johnson had spoiled her for any other man.

CHAPTER EIGHT

Tolu was back in Lagos and found life so dull there. He had employment at the University Teaching Hospital and was back in general practice, but his social life was zero. He didn't see much of his friends, and he made it clear to his mother that he preferred to arrange his own entertainment and leisure. Since he came back, he had had two quarrels with her about Folake Cadmus, who (his mother insisted) was very keen on him.

"But you are not giving her the go-ahead, Tolu," she had lamented.

"I don't love her," Tolu had declared.

"What is this love you keep on about, Tolu? What has that girl got that Folake hasn't got? In fact, if anything, Folake is..."

"I'll tell you this once and for all," Tolu had cut in hotly. "Because of you, Tokoni Beaton has left me. Listen carefully. After today, I don't want to talk about this matter anymore. If I can't marry Tokoni, then I shan't marry anybody. That's my final word on the matter."

His mother had seen the determined look on his face and had let the matter drop, and they had not talked about it again.

Tonight he was thinking of that little boy in his ward who was admitted because he had fallen down from a tree and damaged his spine. He lay flat and inert all the time and was so moody and cheerless that none of the other patients in the ward made friends with him. He hardly ever spoke and looked so forlorn and miserable that Tolu always carried with him a picture of unrelieved gloom after visiting him. The consultant on his case had said the boy would have an operation soon, but he wanted him to have a cheerful and positive disposition before embarking on anything like that. It was quite obvious that the boy was frightened. His parents had separated just recently, and according to the nurses in the ward, they were barely civil to each other when they came to visit Efosa. He was sure that their attitude to each other was contributing to their son's sulks and moodiness. For the little boy's sake, he was quite willing to find a way to make those two put their grievances aside and think of the boy first.

A tap on his door broke through his thoughts, and he looked enquiringly towards the door, to find his mother there.

"Tolu, I want to talk to you."

"Come in, Mama," he invited, and when she came in, he had no smile for her on his face as he used to have before all these troubles started. She sat on the bed, as he was occupying the only chair in the room. Both mother and son could see that they had actually become strangers to each other. Tolu had grown so thin that his mother's heart went out to him. She could see that he was pining over Tokoni Beaton. Her husband had noticed it, too, and that was why she was there.

They had both discussed it, and had agreed that Tolu's happiness was what mattered most. After all, he could have done worse than marry a kobokobo. Some of their friends' sons had put two or three girls in the family way and then refused to accept them. Others were high on drugs while their family lived in terror. Tolu had always done them proud. Since he had said he would marry no one else but this Tokoni, then let him do as he liked. After all, he was old enough to know his own mind. She personally would not allow herself even to imagine her only son not marrying. And the Tokoni girl had already wormed her way into Tolu's father's heart by refusing to write to Tolu or communicate with him in any form, all because his parents did not approve.

"It must have taken a lot of courage on her part if she loves him as much as he claims she does. The girl must have a steadfast character, quiet though she looks," his father had philosophized.

She looked round Tolu's room and took in a deep breath. Then slowly, she said what she had come to say. "Tolu, your father and I have been thinking seriously about you and Tokoni Beaton. We now see that, unless you are allowed to marry her, you will not be happy. To have done what she did must have cost her a lot of heartache, I know. We can see you both love each other very much, so send for her and tell her we have consented to your engagement and marriage."

Tolu stared unbelievingly at his mother as she went on, "You must help me to apologize to her mother, too, for all I said to her on the phone that day. Please forgive us, Tolu, and try to be your cheerful old self again. Seeing you like this has nearly killed us. We love you and want you to be happy always, my son."

"Mama! You don't mean it! Do you say I can marry Tokoni with your full consent? You will welcome her into the family?" Tolu asked.

"Yes, of course," his mother nodded. "You know I don't mince words. It's what your father and I have decided. We want to see you happy, laughing and carefree again."

Tolu could not believe he was hearing his mother rightly. Maybe there was something wrong with his ears. This just couldn't be true. "Oh, Mama, thank you very much! Don't worry, I'll be my old self again, I promise you that. You've made me so happy, I love you both too, you know that," Tolu cried happily. He got up from his chair, carried his mother, a petite woman, up and danced joyfully round the room.

"Eh, put me down!" his mother laughed, banging him on his back.

He went out that evening and told Akin who was very happy too.

Akin said it called for a celebration. Tolu

agreed with him but he had to go and tell Tokoni's mother first, he added.

Marie Beaton was busy ironing. She had been working all day, tidying the house up, rearranging everything, and now she was very tired. "But you must finish the ironing and bake some cakes before resting," she told herself firmly. It was at such times that she missed her daughter most. Tokoni would have helped her with the ironing while she did the baking. Elaye and Pere were coming home today and she wanted to get everything ready for their stay. She could have left the ironing for either of them, but she felt they needed some rest after all their studies. It was not fair to give them chores to do on their first day at home. She was still thinking about them when the doorbell rang. She went to open the door, expecting to see either Elaye or Pere at the door and wondering why they did not use their key and how come they arrived so early. She was surprised to see Tolu and his friend Akinola there. She had a good memory and was very good at remembering faces, so she recognized Akinola as soon as she saw him and remembered him as one of Tolu's best friends. She greeted them both warmly and ushered them in. She had seen Tolu only once since he came back to Lagos. He had looked so sad then, but today, he was as cheerful as ever, radiating happiness.

"How are you, Tolu, and how's everything going? What can I offer you both?" Mrs. Beaton asked kindly, as they sat down.

"Beer for both of us, please, Ma," Tolu replied.

Mrs. Beaton brought out two bottles of beer and set them on low stools beside them. They both thanked her, and when she made as if to bring more, they said, "These will do," as they were not going to stay long.

Mrs. Beaton sat down too, guessing they had come for a very important reason and tried to make small talk while they got themselves composed. "Have you got a steady now, playboy?" she teased Akin. "I can remember being told you didn't have one."

"Yes, I've got one now, and we are getting married in December. We haven't fixed a date yet, though," Akin answered laughing. "And I'd like Toks to be at our wedding. Please tell her that Lolade Dawodu will soon become Mrs. Majekodunmi."

"Oh, good for you! Congratulations!" Mrs. Beaton said, "I'll tell her."

"Mrs. Beaton," Tolu began, "this is one of my happiest days—my happiest day in fact in almost a year. My parents have agreed that I can marry Tokoni. They have agreed to welcome her into the family. My mother told me this afternoon. And she said she is sorry about that phone call she made to you. Can I have her address so that I can write to her and tell her?"

"Oh, Tolu! This is wonderful news. I'm happy for you. I'm sure Tokoni will be delighted too, but I'm sorry I can't give you her address yet. You know

Tokoni. She'd be furious. I will tell her and whatever she says, I will tell you."

Tolu's face fell. He was deeply disappointed, but as Mrs. Beaton said, he knew Tokoni. He had waited so long that it wouldn't hurt him to wait just a little longer.

Elaye arrived while they were still there. She came in shouting, "Mummy, I'm home!" and was running into the kitchen, when she saw they had visitors. She stopped dead in her tracks and greeted them, then she hugged her mother affectionately. She was beside herself with joy when they told her of the reason for their visit.

Pere came in just as they were leaving, and he was delighted about the news too. After Tolu and Akin had gone, Elaye insisted on Tokoni being told that very night, and Pere agreed with her. So their mother tried to call Port Harcourt, but the lines were not through until some two hours later. By this time, it was quite late.

It was Tokoni herself who answered. Her grandparents were already asleep, and she was awake only because she was watching a program she was particularly fond of. She wondered who could be ringing them so late and was surprised to hear her mother's voice on the other end of the line.

"Mummy! Why are you phoning at this time? It's not Sunday yet. I hope there's nothing wrong?" she asked anxiously, her heartbeats quickening.

"There's nothing wrong, my dear. All is well. It's only that I have good news for you. How are Ina and Dada? Are they asleep?" her mother asked her.

"Yes. You know what early birds they are. They went to bed over an hour ago. It must be terribly good news that can't wait until Sunday," Tokoni said. "Elaye and Pere—are they all right?"

"They are fine, and it's on their insistence that I'm calling you so late. They are very happy about this. They would have spoken to you, only this call was not through in time, and now they've gone to a party. They will speak to you on Sunday."

"The news, Mummy, the news!" Tokoni cut in impatiently.

"Well, my dear," laughed her mother, "congrats! Tolu's parents have at last agreed to you two getting married. They are not going to stand in your way anymore. You can make your engagement official and get married as soon as you like. Tolu is beside himself with joy. He came here with Akin. Akin, too, is getting married, to Lolade Dawodu, I think he said, in December, and he wants you to be there. I've been talking so much that I haven't given you a chance to talk. Well now?" finished Mrs. Beaton.

Tokoni held on tightly to the receiver. She had listened in silence while her mother talked. She could not believe her ears, and even after her mother finished talking, she said nothing.

"Tokoni? Can you hear me?" her mother asked anxiously.

"Yes, Mummy," Tokoni replied, her voice coming very faintly to her mother.

"Did you hear all I said?"

"Yes, Mummy. I heard everything."

"Well, say something then!" It was her mother's turn to be impatient.

"Mummy, I'm not sure I heard you right. You mean Tolu's people have accepted me?"

"Right!" her mother laughed.

"Oh, I'm so happy! I can't believe it. I'm so very happy. Is it really true?"

"Yes, Tolu's mother told him. He looked so much happier than the last time I saw him. He wanted your address, but I said I ought to ask you first. What happens now?" Mrs. Beaton wanted to know.

"I don't know. I want some time to think. I'd like to search my mind and see if I'll be able to stand them in future, especially his mother. You know, I can't believe they have accepted me as a person in my own right. They are only doing this for their son's sake, to make him happy. I have a feeling the going will still be rough," Tokoni explained and added, when her mother said nothing, "I hope you know what I mean?"

"Of course I understand, but don't make the waiting too long for him. Tolu assured me they will welcome you, and this is one step forward. By God's grace, you'll conquer all other obstacles. Good night, my dear, and good luck to you," her mother advised her. "Oh, say me well to Ina and Dada," she added.

"Good night, Mummy. Thank you for everything. Give my love to Elaye, Pere... and Tolu."

Tokoni was so happy that she could not sleep straight away, tired though she was. One thing was clear in her mind. She had to wait until she started her leave in eight weeks' time before deciding what to do. She knew it wasn't going to be sweetness and light with Tolu's parents yet, but as her mother said, this was one step forward—a step in the right direction. She thanked God for this stepping-stone and told herself that it was possible Tolu's parents might come to like her in the future.

Tolu was surprised when Mrs. Beaton told him of Tokoni's decision. He wondered what was happening. What did she want to think about? She either wanted to marry him or not, as far as he saw it. She probably was not sure if she still loved him, but she did not talk about there being anyone else on the line, so he was prepared to wait however long she needed to make up her mind. He decided not to bother her by writing her or anything like that anymore.

A little over a month later, he got a birthday card from her. It was a very big card with sincere, simple words, and she had written in it, *"All the love in my heart, Tokoni."* That had been enough to raise his hopes high. It had been like the voice of Hope in Pandora's box and had given him the assurance that all would be well. He also got a card from Jummai Luka, his Youth Service Corps girlfriend. Jummai was such an undemanding girl. He missed her too and the little things she used to do for him. She had nearly cried when he had to leave. He had promised to write to her and thank her for all her help but had not got round to doing so.

"I hope things have worked out between you and your fiancée now," she wrote. "I knew all the time even though you told me nothing about her."

That was true. He had never said a word about Tokoni. How on earth did she know, he wondered.

He decided to write to both of them. He wrote to Jummai first, apologizing for not writing since he came back to Lagos, and thanked her for all she did for him. Then he wrote the more difficult letter and asked Tokoni why she still refused to let him know her address. He asked her if it all meant she loved him no more.

They had at least got his parents' approval. What else was holding her back? Then he asked her to telephone Akin and tell him how she felt, if she still would not write to him.

Tokoni did not know what to do. She had felt she was doing the right thing, but now she was not so sure. Her mother had reproached her, declaring that she was going too far with the whole thing. Ina and Nkechi felt the same too. None of them had realized until now that Tokoni could be as obstinate as a mule. This was getting too much. The poor boy at least deserved to know her address, they argued.

As for Elaye, she just didn't want to hear about it. "I could never have believed you could be so cruel," she had snapped at Tokoni the other day on the phone. "Tolu's parents haven't just passively consented. They have positively agreed to welcome you. He said so himself. What else must he do before you write to him? Have his parents to come to Port Harcourt and beg you on their knees? There is a limit to human endurance. Tolu is only human. The way you are treating him, you will push him into someone else's arms. If he falls for someone else now, you will have only yourself to blame!"

Tokoni heard all these things out before arguing unsuccessfully with her sister about not deciding anything until she was on leave. In the end, Elaye gave up, annoyed. Tokoni was confused, but she just had to be sure. Would she have enough courage to face any more opposition that might arise if she got married to Tolu? It frightened her to remember how quickly their relationship had deteriorated when his parents first objected. Is that the way things would always go between them, whenever there was any conflict with his parents? She needed to think more about this.

However, she telephoned Akin Majekodunmi, as Tolu requested. For the first few minutes of the conversation, they talked about her health and everybody they both knew, except Tolu.

"I heard you are tired of playing the field, Akin?" Tokoni teased him.

"Yes. I'm going to be a respectable married man soon," Akin laughed along with her.

"So it's Lolade. How's she?"

"Yes, it's Lolade, and she is just fine. She is pregnant, you see, so we really must get married in December, before she starts showing too much," Akin explained.

"Well, you are lucky. Say me well to her. Congratulations!" Tokoni said.

"So what about my friend?"

"I love him as much as ever," she whispered.

"Only I just don't know what to do just yet."

"Shall I tell him you still care?" Akin asked.

"Yes, oh, yes, Akin. Please do."

CHAPTER NINE

Events were to make Tokoni's decision for her. It was October 24th, the weekend before she was due to start her one month's leave. She was plaiting Ina's hair when the telephone rang.

Her grandfather answered the call, and she heard him say, "Marie! Do! How are my children? You want to speak to Tokoni? She is plaiting Ina's hair. Hold on. I'll get her."

Tokoni was surprised. Her mother had said she was not going to phone anymore until Tokoni decided what she would do with her month's leave. Tokoni had now decided she would go to Lagos but had told her grandmother only the day before. Then she would see how things were with Tolu's family. That would be the deciding factor. If she had to stay in Lagos, she would miss her grandparents very much, she was sure, but this was not where she belonged. She had missed her mother, Elaye, Tolu, Pere, her friends, and Lagos itself even more.

"Dada, keep talking to her while I finish this one. It's the last one, and you know how tough Ina's hair is," Tokoni called to her grandfather.

When she finished, she took the phone from him. "Hello, Mummy! So you can't wait to hear my voice?"

"My dear, I'm afraid I have bad news for you. Tolu had a car accident yesterday, and he has been in a bad way. He is conscious now, but they say he was terribly lucky to survive.

His mother wants you to come see him, at least to keep him calm and give him a better chance of recovery."

"Oh, my God!" cried Tokoni. "Mummy, is he dying?"

"No, he is not. But he was knocked about pretty badly. His mother came to see me, and she was quite nice. She asked me to beg you to come quickly. It looks as if in her grief, she has understood what you mean to her son. She was crying and asked me to forgive her. I was so touched."

"Mummy, I'll see if I can come on the afternoon flight. If she calls again, tell her I'm on my way. Bye bye." Tokoni said hurriedly.

Her grandfather had already told his wife what happened, so by the time Tokoni finished talking, her grandmother was busy packing her things for her.

"I knew you'd want to leave immediately. It's a good thing you can buy a ticket at the airport these days. I only hope the next flight won't be fully booked. I've put some water on the fire for you."

Tokoni was grateful for her grandmother's help. She herself did not know what to do first. She could not eat. She could not pack. Her mind was in such a turmoil, but her grandmother insisted that she must take something and made her eat some eba. It tasted like sawdust in Tokoni's mouth, but she swallowed it all the same to keep her going. By the time she got herself ready and her things together, it was time to leave. Her grandparents gave her presents to take to her mother, brother, and sister. They both said they would miss her and that she was to enjoy her stay in Lagos and wished both Tolu and her all the best. They both went with her to the airport and waited until the plane took off.

"That girl will make some man a very good wife," her grandmother said, and her husband nodded in silent agreement.

During the flight, Tokoni's mind worked like a clock. She kept thinking about Tolu and what her stubbornness had done to him. She wondered if she had done the right thing by him after all. She would make it up to him, she vowed, only let the Lord just spare him, for his parents' sake, if not for her own. She did not know how she could live if Tolu died. Nobody came to meet her at the airport, so she took a taxi home.

Her mother, Elaye, and Pere, who were all at home, were very happy to see her. They asked after Ina, Dada, and all their relatives. They talked about their presents, biding their time and avoiding any talk about the accident. Then Tokoni asked which hospital Tolu was in.

"At the L.U.T.H. They took him there

naturally," her mother explained. "Pere can take you if you want to go right away. But have you eaten?"

"Yes, I ate before I left. I must go now. You don't know how my mind has been working. I was thinking what I'd do if he died. He is not dying?" Tokoni asked, wishing to be reassured.

"Of course he isn't, Toks. Your presence is all the tonic he needs. Anyway, it's nearly visiting time. It's 4 o'clock now, and in another hour and a half, there'll be loads of visitors. You don't want to rush, do you?"

"If Tolu dies, I will never forgive myself for trying him so much," Tokoni said brokenly.

Elaye went to her and put her arms around her elder sister, saying comfortingly, "He'll be all right, Toks. You'll see. You go along now. Pere, come on, o."

"Right!" Pere said, waving the car keys as they said goodbye and went out.

"Give our love to him," Elaye called.

The traffic was smooth, and they did not say much on the drive to the hospital. Pere knew his sister did not feel like talking, so he respected that fact. They got there in no time at all, but the nurses would not let them go in and see him, as they had instructions to allow only his family. Tokoni told them she was his girlfriend, but they insisted she had to wait till his parents came and gave their consent.

They waited for about fifteen minutes before Tolu's parents arrived. They were genuinely pleased to see her and told the nurses the young lady was his fiancée whom he'd been asking for.

The nurses were surprised and apologetic. "Oh, sorry, miss, but why didn't you say so? She said she was his girlfriend, and we thought she was just a casual friend," they apologized, all concerned.

Pere excused himself to go and see a friend at the Nurses' Hostel. He did not wish to witness the emotional reunion of Tolu and Tokoni. Their story always touched a soft spot in him, and he was not ready to grow sentimental today. He had already been to see Tolu, and he knew how the poor guy was. Tolu was in a private room. They went into the room, but he was sleeping, so his parents sat down. They started making some polite enquiries about how she had fared in Port Harcourt, her relatives, health, and work. They asked her if she would be going back. She said she didn't know yet. Tolu's mother could see that Tokoni was nervous, so she started telling her how the accident had really happened. Tokoni was looking so intently at Tolu's bandaged head. It was bandaged so that only his face showed. His left arm was in plaster.

"It was at Ojuelegba roundabout here," Mrs. Johnson explained. "A reckless danfo driver had overtaken on a bend and ran straight into him. He has head injuries, a broken arm, broken ribs, and some internal damage, but nothing permanent. He was on the danger list, but he will pull through, thank God. It's a miracle he is even alive."

Tolu's father said nothing. He looked as calm
as if nothing had happened. Tokoni looked again at
Tolu's sleeping face, pale and listless in the coolness
of the room. One of his closed eyes was swollen
and black. Across his brow and cheeks were patches
of black stitches. Despite that, he still looked as
handsome as she knew him. She stood at the head
of the bed and looked down at him, her heart full of
love and prayer. She never had been able to say
much in front of his parents, so she just stood there,
looking lovingly at him and praying for him.

Tolu suddenly opened his eyes and looked at
his parents. There was the spark of life in them.

"Tolulope, Ajani Okin, my child. Don't worry.
You'll get well, my son. You pull your weight and
you will get better." Then his mother started
chanting his Oriki—his praises. Ajani was Tolu's
praise-name, and Okin, which is the Yoruba name
for the Peacock, his totem. The Yoruba all have
Oriki, which their elders chant whenever the person
in question has done something praiseworthy or is
in trouble and needs encouragement.

"Tokoni? Have you told her?" he asked and
winced with pain.

His parents both nodded together and looked at
Tokoni. She moved from her position to the side of
the bed, where he could see her well. "Yes, Tolu,
and I'm here."

Tolu's father got up from the low stool by the
bedside and stood at the foot of the bed. Tolu stared

at Tokoni then he blinked and looked at her again. "Toks, you are back?" he asked, his voice so faint she could hardly hear him.

"Yes, and I'll stay with you as long as you need me, my darling. You just try and get well for all our sakes," Tokoni said.

Tolu's normally strong hands lay limply on the bed cover. He held out his one good arm, the right one, to her, and she took it in both her hands. Then she bent down and kissed him on the forehead. His parents went out quietly, saying they would come back later. Tolu could not say much. He just kept repeating, "Toks, you are really back!" over and over again, and with his hand still in hers, he fell asleep.

Every day after that, she came to see him, and as he got better, they talked about their problems. His parents softened towards her and started to know what sort of girl she really was during this trying period.

Four weeks later, Tolu was back at home, and Tokoni had applied to be transferred back to Lagos because she was getting married. Her director was marvelous, so it was granted quickly.

It was December already, and the wedding was fixed for the last Saturday in March to coincide with Tokoni's birthday. Both mothers were disappointed. They complained to each other that they had wanted to make it a big affair, but that date was too soon for them. Tokoni and Tolu had decided that three months was enough notice to give their respective parents. They had waited too long. They weren't prepared to wait much longer before becoming man and wife.

Akin and Lolade were married on December 18th. Then Tolu and Tokoni started to make their own preparations. Elaye would be Tokoni's chief bridesmaid. Tokoni was going to have a long bridal train, much to her chagrin, but there were so many cousins and relatives who just had to be chosen. The lovely dresses were designed and sewn by Latoya Fashions.

Tolu and Tokoni started house-hunting soon after he came out of the hospital, and it was like looking for a place in Heaven. There just were not enough houses to go round for every married couple in Lagos. They were about to give up hope when they got news of a recently vacated flat in the married Resident Doctors' quarters at Tolu's hospital. It was not in line with what they wanted, but the two bedrooms were large enough, and when they'd finished decorating it to their taste, it looked great. Tolu moved in.

Since the bride was not Yoruba, Tolu's parents decided that there was no point in presenting her and her family with the traditional engagement gifts. It was going to be a very awkward situation otherwise, as Mrs. Beaton and her relations would not know how to receive the engagement bearers. So this was omitted, and everything had to be done the bride's way.

A month before the wedding, Tokoni was "excised" in the Ijaw traditional way. Then she was dressed in a velvet wrapper, which she tied over her breasts down to just above her knees. She had coral beads round her neck, on her wrists, and on her knees, and red powder on her feet. On the first day, a lot of people came to see her, including Tolu's parents. They did not think much of the excision but had not objected because, according to them, "tradition was tradition." Mrs. Johnson even told Mrs. Beaton that formerly it used to be practiced in her family too. Her cousins' wives and some relatives came every day, and they all danced and made merry. Tokoni even had a lady-in-waiting and received many presents. Tolu teased her no end about what he still called their "primitive custom," but she didn't mind. There was no longer any venom in his voice.

Then it was time for Tolu's family to come for the engagement and pay the dowry. They were given a long list of things to bring for their bride which included two pairs of George materials, two pairs of Abada materials, two handbags, two pairs of shoes, a suitcase, an umbrella, and some other things which they knew or thought their bride would need. Tolu's family came with all these things and were welcomed by Tokoni's family, who served them drinks and asked them the reason for their visit. Tolu's people then presented their case in English and brought drinks for everybody. Then they ate, and it was time to pay the bride price of fifty naira. A senior member of the Beatons' family suggested that as the bride was educated, the bride price should be more than the usual amount, but here both Marie and Tokoni put their foot down. The money and the gifts were then collected, and Tokoni and Tolu both knelt before Tokoni's uncle and were blessed.

The marriage at All Saints Church was a beautiful ceremony. Tokoni's grandparents and most of their relations came all the way from Port Harcourt. Her father's sisters came too, and their house was packed full. The guests were superbly dressed. The groom's family turned up gorgeously in Alaari or Sanyan aso oke with lace bubas. The bride's people were in George or Kente, and the women had pretty lace blouses. It was a combination of traditional and Western-styled costumes, all blending together.

"You look a dream. How I wish I were young again. I would have eloped," her grandfather said.

At 9 p.m., Tolu's people came to take Tokoni home.

Tokoni wept. She wept because she was going to live in a completely new environment with a new set of people, but mostly she wept because of the heart-rending advice given to her by her grandfather.

"You will be mistress of a household now," he told her. "You must learn to solve your problems. You must not come running to your mother with them as before. For better or for worse, you must stick to your husband."

His expression contradicted the severity of his words, but still Tokoni wept.

"You are marking a stage in your life," he added, "and stepping into another stage, which calls for higher responsibility and a sense of maturity. You must not let a third party know whatever private thing happens between you, within the four walls of your home. Some of your friends will tell you their husbands do this and that and buy all sorts of things for them and are so good to them that they never quarrel. Don't listen to such people. Half of the things they tell you are not true. If, for one reason or another, your husband cannot afford to meet a request, give him time. Don't make him feel unimportant. Take him into consideration on all matters. You are marrying the man of your choice. No one forced him on you, so you must always do those things that made him decide to marry you. You are a stranger in your mother's house from today."

Tokoni nodded, whispered assent, and went off with Tolu's people.